TRAGIC SECRETS

A HOLIDAY ROMANCE (ISLAND OF LOVE
BOOK TWO)

MICHELLE LOVE

HOT AND STEAMY ROMANCE

CONTENTS

Blurb   v

1. Chapter One   1
2. Chapter 2   8
3. Chapter 3   15
4. Chapter 4   21
5. Chapter 5   27
6. Chapter 6   33
7. Chapter 7   39
8. Chapter 8   45
9. Chapter 9   51
10. Chapter 10   57
11. Chapter 11   64
12. Chapter 12   70
13. Chapter 13   76
14. Chapter 14   83
15. Chapter 15   89
16. Chapter 16   95
17. Chapter 17   101
18. Chapter 18   107
19. Chapter 19   113
20. Chapter 20   119
21. Chapter 21   124
22. Chapter 22   130
23. Chapter 23   136
24. Chapter 24   142
25. Chapter 25   148
26. Chapter 26   154
27. Chapter 27   161
28. Chapter 28   168
29. Chapter 29   174
30. Chapter 30   180

Made in "The United States" by:

Michelle Love

© Copyright 2020

ISBN: 978-1-64808-711-0

✿ Created with Vellum

BLURB

**It was supposed to be a time of mourning, reflection, and endings.
Instead I found love, happiness, and new beginnings...**
She'd caught my eye right from the start.
That little filly was as wild as they come, though.
Friends. That was her favorite word.
I wanted more, and I always get what I want.
But with her, love had to come first.
Her virginity meant a lot to her.
She meant a lot to me.
And just as it started coming together, it all came crashing down.
Why, I didn't know.
We were in love.
Or had it all just been a crazy game to her?

**I was there to make money—nothing more than that. Then that
cowboy showed up, making things heat up inside me...**
Boots, cowboy hat, blue jeans that fit him like a glove; that man made
my mouth water the second I saw him.
His hands, even though calloused from hard work on his family's
ranch, moved over my skin like silk.

I'd thought I wanted him kept at a distance—as my friend—but my heart and body wanted much more than that.

I was sure my goofy ways had him looking at me more like a little sister than a love interest.

And I required love—long term love—if I was to give my well-kept virginity to the cowboy.

Everything was right as rain for us. The passion we shared was beyond anything I'd ever dreamed of—until I got one phone call that knocked us off our path.

Would he move on or would he wait for me? I had no way of knowing...

1

CHAPTER ONE

Pitt

Mornings at the ranch never failed to amaze me. Pinks, yellows, purples, and blues mixed with the snowy white mountain peaks of the Rockies that surrounded our land; that's the view that greeted my eyes each sunrise.

Nestled between those mountains, our two-thousand-acre spread was home to six-hundred cattle, fifteen horses, three dogs, five cats, twenty chickens, and our family.

Leaning on the horn of my grandpa's saddle that had been handed down to me, I gazed at the horizon as the cattle began their day of grazing in the back pasture. Old Pete, one of our oldest geldings, had greeted me in the horse barn that morning, and his soft neigh persuaded me pick him to be my companion and coworker for the day.

"Pete, would ya' look at that?" I always talked to our animals like they were people. When you grow up surrounded by them, they have a tendency to become friends. "Five minutes ago it was dark and cold out here. Now look how beautiful and light it is. I wouldn't want to live anywhere else in this whole world, Pete. How 'bout you?"

He softly neighed his agreement; I understood him completely.

"Yep, I thought that's what you'd say." Sighing as I took in all the grandeur, I watched as the sun's light began to fill first one crevice in the mountains and then another and another until the whole mountain range lit up. "This never gets old. Does it, Pete?"

The horse blew out through his nostrils, letting me know he once again agreed with me.

"Time to head to the lodge for breakfast. Cookie will have the coffee and hotcakes ready for me and all the other guys. I'll get you a big ol' cup of oats and some fresh water, too." Moving my right leg a bit to put slight pressure on his ribcage, I pulled the reins to turn him around so we could head home for a couple of hours before coming back out to check on the herd.

My mind always wandered during the ride back home, and like so many other mornings, it settled on thoughts of my father. We'd lost him to lung cancer a little over a year ago, and I was beginning to wonder when it would stop hurting.

Mom seemed to be doing better with the loss than I was. Not that I was bedridden with grief or anything like that. Working on a ranch didn't give a man much time to wallow in sorrow. Cattle still needed to be fed, watered, doctored, and watched, after all.

Dad hadn't been a rancher—a fact my grandpa, my mom's father, didn't much care for. In the beginning, he didn't care for my father much at all, so the story goes. Dad married Chester Brewer's twenty-one-year-old daughter, Fannie Brewer, behind the rancher's back.

At first, Grandpa had disowned Mom, who'd already been warned of such an eventuality if she went against his wishes and married Jody Zycan. My father had been an inventor even then, though he hadn't yet struck it rich. He made a modest living working for his uncle as a car salesman. His passion was engines, though, and he revised and reworked them until he could make one purr like a kitten while being as powerful as a lion.

For two years my mother and father lived in a small house inside the Gunnison, Colorado, city limits. Chester Brewer's ranch, Pipe Creek, lay on the outskirts of town.

I was born in that little house thirty-two years ago. One day during my childhood a young man showed up to meet my father. Galen Dunne had heard word of my father's knack with engines and asked him if he'd like to collaborate on a marine engine he wanted to make.

Dad agreed. One thing led to another. The engines he helped create were sold to the United States military. Galen Dunne had helped make my father into a billionaire.

Jody Zycan had finally earned Chester Brewer's respect—and a place on his ranch, the place my mother felt most at home. Dad and Mom built a sprawling ranch-mansion, as my grandpa called it, in the southernmost corner of the two-thousand acres. They also had three more babies—my three little sisters—two who followed the ranching side of the family and one who followed my father's inventing ways.

Lucy took care of the chickens, Janice took care of the dogs and cats, and we all took care of the cattle. The youngest, Harper, was in town attending Western State Colorado University, studying physics. We didn't see much of her as she kept her head in the books or was at some lab doing experiments most of the time.

As I approached the barn, I saw that everyone had converged there, putting horses away and getting ready to head in to eat breakfast at the original house my grandpa had built. Janice came out of the feed room, dragging an enormous bag of dog food behind her.

"Mice have taken over the feed room from my dogs and cats, Pitt." She blew a chunk of dark hair out of her blue eyes. "Think you can help me set out traps after breakfast?"

"I think I can do that for ya', sis." I climbed off Old Pete and led him into a stall to give him his breakfast. "So, this mornin' ain't been too good to ya', huh?"

With a roll of her eyes, she huffed, "Not at all. First, I opened the barn door and out ran a raccoon. He scooted right over my boot, and I jumped fifty feet into the air, screamin' like a banshee."

"Fifty feet!" I teased her as I filled Old Pete's water bucket. "I guess we got us an Olympic star on our hands now, don't we, Pete?" Patting him on the head, I swore the old gelding smiled at me.

Janice tugged the heavy bag outside while snarling at me. "It was very high, I can promise you that, Pitt. And ain't it about time to retire that damn straw hat you got on? Dad threw that thing out three years ago. How'd ya' even find it?"

Pulling the hat off, I looked at it. "I found it in the toolbox in the back of the four-wheeler when I took it over to Grandpa's this morning. I figured I'd wear it today and think about Dad."

"Don't you think that'll make you sad, Bubba?" Janice asked, looking a little concerned. "You don't want to cry out there in front of the cows, now do ya'?"

"Nah," I said with a grin as I put the cowboy hat back on top of my head. "Big strong cowboys like me don't cry, little sis. And I like to remember Dad." I walked over to her, taking the bag out of her struggling hands, then draping it over my shoulder. "Where is it you want this?"

She smiled and pointed at the back of the four-wheeler she'd driven over. "On the back of that, please, and thank you very much."

The other three ranch hands came up to the barn, heading inside after tipping their hats to my sister. "Mornin', Miss Janice," they all said in unison.

"Mornin', boys," my little sister called out to them. "See y'all at the breakfast table." She nudged me with her shoulder. "Beaux Foster certainly is growing up to be a handsome man, isn't he?"

Tossing the dog food onto the back of the four-wheeler, I nodded and said with mock enthusiasm, "Oh, girl! He is, right?" I made a high-pitched giggle, then tossed my little sister over my shoulder. "You are such a freak, Janice. Those boys should be more like brothers to you, not potential boy toys."

"I'm only a year older than him. He's already twenty-four, you know." She pounded my back with her little fists. She may twenty-five, but she'd always been a tiny thing. "Pitt, put me down! I don't want them to see me like this." Her cowboy hat fell off, and I put her back on her feet so she could retrieve it to cover up the mop of dark curls that had spilled out from underneath it.

"Shit, Janice," I said as I laughed. "Did you even brush that hair before you put that thing on and came on out here?"

"Hush up, now." She tucked her unruly curls back under her hat, then hurried inside.

The cowhands came out of the barn, surrounding Lucy, one of my other sisters.

"Let me get that bucket for ya', Miss Lucy," Joe Lamb said as he grabbed the bucket she'd used to carry the chicken feed.

"Thank you, John," Lucy said as she batted her green eyes at him. "Such a gentleman, you are."

The youngest of the hired hands at a tender twenty-years old, Rick Savage shoved his hand through thick blonde hair after taking off his hat and using it to swat the nearby Beaux on the ass. "There's a lady present, Beaux. Get that hat off your head."

The three young men all had eyes for my way-too-old-for-them sister. At twenty-nine, my sister had yet to find Mr. Right. It was my opinion that all three of the much younger men who hovered around her didn't have a chance in hell. Lucy had never been the easiest to get along with—but maybe that was part of the appeal to these young pups.

Lucy wrinkled her nose as she looked at me. "Pitt Zycan, where did you find that awful hat?"

I took the stained, bent, and somewhat holey straw hat off and held it out to her. "I found it in the toolbox on the back of the four-wheeler I drove over here this mornin'. It belonged to Dad."

"Well, that doesn't mean you should be wearin' it. You look like a damn fool." Lucy walked past me as Rick opened the screen door for her.

John moved fast to get right behind Lucy. "Thanks, Rick."

"You dick," Rick hissed as he went in behind him, leaving Beaux and me with a slamming screen door in our faces.

Beaux grabbed the handle before it closed all the way. "Jackasses."

"I agree." I followed him inside, stopping to hang my hat on the hat tree just inside the door.

The smell of coffee led me like a cartoon character into the kitchen, which bustled with activity as Cookie moved around, trying to get everything on the table as everyone helped themselves to coffee, juice, or milk.

I stood back for a moment to take everything in. My life had been so full with work and all these people that I'd had little to no time to do much grieving over my father.

The truth was that I'd shut down, emotionally speaking. For the most part, I was there for my family, but I'd lost myself along the way.

Trying to maintain a happy-go-lucky attitude for Mom and my sisters, I never took the time to reflect on how my father's loss affected me. I'd stopped dating. I'd ended things with my long-time girl, Tanya Waters, only a month after my father found out he had cancer. That had been two years ago.

For two years, I'd been alone. No dating. Nothing.

Man, what the hell happened to you, Pitt Zycan?

After breakfast and a short nap, I woke up to a knock on my bedroom door. "Pitt, it's Mom. Galen Dunne is on the phone for you."

Getting out of bed, I went to the hallway to pick up the landline phone, my mother nowhere to be seen. "Hey Galen. How're things goin'?"

"Well," he answered me in his lilting Irish accent. "Look, I don't want ya' to be gettin' mad at your mother, Pitt."

"What would I be gettin' mad at her for?" I replied, confused.

"For callin' me and tellin' me that you're in need of some time to get your life back in order." He sighed. "It's been over a year since your father passed. I wouldn't be much of a friend to the man if I didn't try to help ya' get on with your life, now would I?"

I wasn't opposed to figuring out how to get back to being myself. "And just what do you suggest I do, Galen?"

"Come to my island resort, Paradise. Be my guest for the next three months. It's all on the house. I'll take care of all the arrangements. All you have to do is pack and get on your jet. Have it take you to Aruba, and I'll take it from there. And I'm not really askin' ya'. I'm tellin' ya'. You're coming for a long visit. Your dad would want you to do this."

I was silent for a moment, thinking it over. What there anything holding me to the ranch for the next few months? "I found an old cowboy hat of his today, Galen." I thought that might've been an omen. I wasn't usually one to look for meaning in small things, but something felt different this time. "I'll head out tomorrow."

"Good," he sounded happy that I'd agreed so easily. "See ya' soon, Pitt."

Well, this should be interesting—a cowboy in Paradise.

CHAPTER 2

Kaylee

"If I told you that you have a beautiful body, would you hold it against me?" I rolled my eyes at the wannabe Lothario as I placed his fifth beer on the bar in front of him.

I pointed over his shoulder. "Isn't that your girl over there, cowboy? I doubt she'd like the question you've just asked me."

"Oh?" He looked back at the blonde who sat at the table he'd been sitting at all night. "She's not my girl. She's my...cousin. Yeah, she's just my cousin. I felt sorry for her 'cause she was home all alone, and I asked her if she wanted to tag along with me. I'm free." He winked one pale green eye at me as he shoved a meaty fist through his auburn curls. "So, back to the question I asked. Would you?"

I'd been working at the same bar on Sixth Street in Austin, Texas, for the last two years. The Dogwood was best known for our creative cocktails and attracted all types of customers. I'd heard every line imaginable and had prepared smartass comebacks for most of them.

"If I tied you up and put you in the trunk of my car and left you there, would you hold it against me, cowboy?" I looked at his beer. It would be the last I'd be serving him; he'd already downed four of them in a matter of two hours. "And that's the last one of those you'll be getting from me. Now go on," I waved my hands at him as if I was shooing an animal away, "Scat."

Picking up his beer, he rolled his eyes. "You're missing out."

"Oh, I know what I'm missing out on." I turned away from him and headed to the back, badly in need of a short break. "Jake, I'm taking ten. The bar's all yours."

"Take twenty," he called out after me. "I heard that exchange you just had and think you need a little more time to regain your usual charming wit."

"Bite me," I hissed as I left the bar through the swinging door at the back of the room.

Tammy, our assistant manager, looked up at me as she tapped away at her computer. "Why are you wearing such a foul expression, Kaylee?"

Flopping down on the chair in front of the desk, I shook my head. "I'm not sure. This dumbass gave me a stupid line, and I just thought about how much I'm over listening to drunken men feeding me pickup lines from the eighties. I mean, can't they come up with anything new?"

"I heard one the other day I hadn't heard before," Tammy said as she grinned and leaned forward. "He said, and I quote, 'I've lost my number, can I have yours?' How cheesy, right?" She laughed, and I joined her.

"Did you give it to him?" I asked, as she'd been known to fall for some of the dudes who frequented the bar.

"Not that night, no." Her cheeks went pink. "But he came around the next night, apologizing. And then I did give him my number, and we went to eat at Denny's after I closed up the bar for the night."

"And after that?" I knew she'd done more than that. Tammy had a rep for being a little free with her charms.

She went back to tapping away at the keyboard. "Mind your business, Kaylee."

"I see," I said with a smile, my suspicions confirmed.

We were silent for a moment as she continued to work at the

computer, and I let my mind wander. "Do you ever get tired of this? Is this where you imagined you'd be at this point in your life?"

Hearing the seriousness in my tone, she looked away from the screen and up at me. "What do you mean? I don't mind this work. I've never been one to be able to sit in an office all day, so this is as good as anything in my books. Why do you ask?"

I nodded my head, understanding where she was coming from. With a big sigh, I let her in on how I'd been feeling lately. "I just wish I could find a calling is all." I'd never been drawn to anything in particular, but I knew working in a bar wasn't all I was meant for. "I took two years of college right after high school to get the basics out of the way. I thought that some career would start calling out to me during that time, and I'd go on to get a degree of some kind to help me get to that career. Only one never called, and I never went on with college. I ended up here. At this bar. Serving assholes."

Shaking her head, Tammy argued, "They're not all assholes, Kaylee. You just never give any guy a chance to show you who he really is."

"Because there's nothing to show." I threw my hands in the air. "I see them out there, Tammy. They go from one girl to the next until they find some poor sucker who believes their shit. Well, I'm not falling for any of it."

With a roll of her eyes, she laid it out for me. "First off, you know this isn't the best spot to be looking for your future spouse; no one's at their best when they're drunk at a bar at last call. Besides, you just need to get laid, girl. That's your biggest problem, and we all know it. And you know Jake would be glad to pop that cherry for you." She winked at me. "He's said so at least a million times since you started working here."

"What?" I could feel my face heat at that information. As if the night could get any worse; now I had to go back out there and work with the guy. "I really need to get a new job. I'm going crazy here."

Pausing, Tammy looked up at the ceiling for a second before looking back at me. "You know, my cousin called me the other day.

She asked me if I wanted to work at one of the bars at this resort she manages."

I leaned forward with anticipation. "And you haven't taken her up on the offer yet?"

"No." Her blonde bob bounced around her shoulders as she shook her head. "It's in the middle of the Caribbean on some remote island. I'm still in school working on my MBA. I can't drop out now."

I could feel the wheels spinning in my head. *A job on an island resort? Sounds like paradise to me!*

"Well, what about me?" I asked as I stood up and started pacing. "You know I've got nothing holding me here; I could totally go do that." I stopped and looked at her. "Wait. What kind of job is it? Just a regular serving job? And where would I live? And how would I get there every day? And—?"

"Chill," she said as she got up and took me by the shoulders. "And take a seat. I'll tell you what she told me."

I took my seat and waited for her to sit back down in her own. "Okay, okay. It's just that it sounds like the exact change of pace I need right now; I'm excited."

"I can see that." She pulled up a website then turned the screen around. "This is The Paradise Resort. You know Galen Dunne, the billionaire? He owns it. And my cousin Camilla runs it for him. She told me that they would pay for airfare to Aruba and then send a yacht to get you from there. Employees stay in staff housing, which is like a hotel room with your own bed and bathroom. There's a central living area and kitchen for everyone to use. And the pay is generous. Plus, there's medical and life insurance as well as a retirement plan."

"A career!" I hopped up again, clapping my hands as I jumped up and down. "A real career, Tammy." Looking at her with hope-filled eyes, I asked, "Would you tell her about me?"

"And tell her what?" she asked as she pulled her glasses off and laid them on the desk. "That you're a great employee until a customer starts flirting?" She shook her head again. "The resort caters to the upper-class—and they would never accept rude behavior, Kaylee."

I knew that the kind of people who would be guests on that island would never be as crass as the drunks who frequented our bar. "I can act like a normal, nice human being when I'm around other normal, nice human beings, Tammy. And you know that I'm a pro when it comes to making cocktails; hell, I've come up with all the best sellers in the past year."

"Sit down," she said, pulling up an application on the site. "I'll help you fill this out and put myself as a reference. In the morning, I'll give Camilla a call to see what she thinks. That's all I can do, Kaylee. But I agree that you need a change. This place will never work out for you in the long run. I can see that. These guys aren't going to change."

"I know it." I sat back down, and we got to work on the application, a grin on my face he whole time.

Later that night I went home to my apartment and dropped onto my twin bed. This might not be my home for much longer. In a few weeks, I might be making drinks for the richest of the rich—movie stars, socialites, CEOs—who knew?

The sound of an island breeze filled my head. The smell of sweet ocean air filled my nose. I closed my eyes, imagining the entire beautiful scene.

The pictures on the website had been gorgeous: swimming pools, overwater bungalows, swaying palm trees, and so much more. The perks for employees ranged from two days off each week to free meals at the resort's restaurants. Food and drinks were even provided at staff housing.

Everything was within walking distance on the island, so no car would be needed. I wouldn't have to bring anything other than my clothing and personal effects. I could sell my furniture and my car, then jump on a plane to Aruba and start a real career in a genuine island paradise.

I fell asleep with all these exciting thoughts filling my head, and the next morning I woke up to the sound of my cell ringing. Rubbing my eyes, I realized I'd fallen asleep with my clothes on. "Damn, girl." Tammy's name glowed on my cell, and I sat up, feeling butterflies swarm my tummy. "Tammy?"

"Yeah, girl," she said. "You up yet? I know it's a bit early, but I thought you might want to hear this right away."

Crossing my fingers, I asked, "Hear what?"

"That Camilla will be calling you in an hour to do a phone interview." She laughed. "She said she'd take my word on you. So, you better not fuck it up by being rude to anyone there. You hear me, Kaylee Simpson?"

"Oh, my God!" I shrieked. "Thank you, thank you, thank you! I swear I'll be on my best behavior! I've gotta get ready for the call." I hopped out of bed. "I need to shower and brush my teeth. Oh, and put on something nice."

"The interview is over the phone, Kaylee." Tammy laughed. "But I get it. Let me know how it goes, and if we need to start looking for your replacement at the bar."

"I will." I tossed the phone on the bed then ran to get myself ready.

At precisely eleven, my cell rang. I picked it up. "Kaylee Simpson. What can I do for you today?" I thought I sounded nice and helpful.

"Hello, this is Camilla Chambers." She hesitated. "You can call me Mrs. Chambers. My cousin Tammy told me about you, and I saw the application you filled out on our website. Tell me why you want to work here and what makes you think you will make a good fit for the resort, Kaylee."

Straight to it, then.

I stood up tall, as if I was actually standing in front of the woman. "I can make excellent cocktails and have memorized most of the *Bartender's Bible*. I love experimenting with new flavors and can make a delicious drink out of pretty much anything. Career-wise, I'm not looking for anything short term. I would give you all I've got to give, and that means making this job my career. I would make a great fit because I would make the island my home and treat my coworkers, management, and the guests like family."

Silence hung in the air for a moment, "Excellent answer," she finally said, and I exhaled a sigh of relief. "How would you like to be the day-shift bartender at our most popular bar, The Cantina Cordova?"

"I would like that very, very much, Mrs. Chambers," I said, hardly able to contain a squeal of delight.

"I'm glad to hear it. I'll get everything arranged and send over an e-mail with the new employee packet, and as soon as you send back the signed documents and accept the salary, I'll send you the travel arrangements. I'll be seeing you very soon, Kaylee Simpson. Bye now."

"Bye," I said as I hugged myself. "And thank you so much, Mrs. Chambers."

Looks like I'm going to Paradise!

CHAPTER 3

Pitt

I hopped on our private jet early the next morning. I'd always been an early riser—that's just a rancher's life—but even still I set off a lot earlier than Galen had thought I would. He was surprised when I called him, telling him I was in Aruba. He sent a yacht to pick me up, and I arrived on the island before daylight.

Galen greeted me personally at the dock that morning. "Welcome to Paradise, Pitt." He clapped me on the back. "It's damn good to see ya'."

"It's good to see you too, Galen." I walked with him as the steward grabbed my luggage from the boat and followed us to the place I'd be staying the next three months. "I haven't seen you since Dad's memorial. And Mom said to tell you hi, too."

"I'll give her a call later." Galen pointed to the row of cabins that sat out over the water—I could barely make them out in the night sky. "The first one is yours. I've got a personal hostess for you. She'll see to your every need."

"No, thanks." I wasn't into being taken care of. "You know I'm not that kind of man, Galen. I wasn't raised like that."

"Well, it's protocol here, Pitt. She'll be able to make your stay here very pleasant." He seemed insistent. "Any questions you have, any activities you need organized—she'll be able to help you out."

I had the feeling he might be trying to set me up. "Galen, that's nice of you. No, thank you, though. You know how it is with me and women. We don't exactly mesh well. I'm not much of a talker, and I'm pretty used to silence. Women don't always understand that. If I need something, I'll ask for it. Don't you worry 'bout me."

With a nod, Galen let the hostess thing go. He knew me well enough to know that when I said *no thank you*, I meant it. "Okay. You've got my number if you need anything, and I'll show you around myself." He opened the door. "This is your bungalow for the next few months. Make it your home away from home, Pitt. It's already been stocked with all sorts of things. Now, I'm going back to the comfort of my bed for a few more hours."

"Cool." I stepped inside, then turned to take my bags from the steward. "Here, let me get those."

"I can come in and put your things away for you, sir," the man said as he held the bags tight.

"Nope." I nodded at Galen. "Tell him I'll be just fine, will ya', Galen?"

Galen laughed and patted the man on the back. "No need to help this one, Jack. He's not one to be catered to."

"Yes, sir." He let go of my things, then the two of them turned and left me.

Not bothering to turn on any lights as I made my way through the dark place, I left the baggage on the sofa and found the glass doors to the patio already open.

Walking out onto the deck, the inviting sound of water lapping underneath the bungalow was instantly soothing. I took a seat on one of the two lounge chairs, then laid back to check out the stars. "Hey there, old friends. No matter where I am, you're always right there, aren't ya'?" Yeah, I talked to the stars, the sun, and the moon like they were people, too.

When you grow up on a ranch, sitting alone, watching over your cattle, you tend to talk to things most people wouldn't even consider having a conversation with.

The quiet comforted me. It eased my mind more than I thought it would.

I hadn't come to meet hot chicks. I hadn't come to fraternize with billionaires. I'd come for one reason.

To finally grieve for my father.

But as I laid there on that lounge chair and looked at those stars, I could practically hear my father's voice. *Boy, you are not here to mourn me. You know damn good and well that I'm fine where I am. Just like I've always been.*

"I know that, you stubborn man," I said out loud. "But I miss you, believe it or not. I miss you, and I miss your stubborn ways."

It's time to start living again, Pitt Zycan. You've been grieving in your own way this whole time.

I couldn't tell if the voice in my head still sounded like my father or if it started to sound more like myself.

Hell, I'd started grieving for Dad before the Lord even came to take him home with him. From the moment I found out he had lung cancer, I mourned.

The only good thing that came out of that was that you quit that Copenhagen habit.

"Well, tobacco killed you, Dad," I remind him—or the him I've been talking to in my mind. And then I felt kind of silly for talking out loud. "I hope no one else is up, sitting on their decks and thinking a lunatic has moved in next door to them."

I closed my eyes, wanting to shut out the sound of his voice. My life had changed drastically the moment my father was diagnosed and even a year after his passing I still hadn't found my footing.

It was time to get on with my life—to break through this fog that had descended over me and get back to living. I wasn't a kid anymore —thirty-two years old and not getting any younger. If the last year had taught me anything, it's that the years were starting to move by faster than ever.

It's time to find yourself a woman. The voice was back, and once again I couldn't distinguish whether it was my own or that of my father's.

Tanya was never the girl for you. That's why you found it so easy to leave her behind. But there is someone out there for you, and I don't want you to be so caught up in missing me that you miss seeing her.

I couldn't deny that. The fact that I was able to let Tanya go so damn easily proved to me that our love wasn't real. Or deep. Or meant to be, either.

I'd known her for so long that things just kind of fell in place without much thought. I'd gone to high school with her and then we'd ended up in the same college. Then she ended up managing the feed store where I bought food for all of our animals. One day, she asked me if I'd like to come over to her place for chicken-fried steaks with homemade mashed potatoes and creamy gravy. She said she'd even throw in some sweet tea.

How could a man pass that up?

One dinner led to another and another until we were dating and having sleepovers at her place. But my heart wasn't ever hers, and hers was never mine. I had to admit that she was a damn good sport when I told her that I didn't have time for a relationship when Dad got sick.

Her exact words were, "I understand, Pitt. You do what you've gotta do, handsome."

As I had walked away from her front door that afternoon, I couldn't help but notice how she never mentioned anything about being there when I got ready to come back. I knew she wouldn't wait around for me, and she was smart enough to know that I wouldn't be back anyway.

I hadn't asked about her after that. I stayed out of the feed store after that, too, leaving that business up to Lucy and her entourage of ranch hands.

I hadn't even seen Tanya once since my father's memorial. She showed up to that, but so did most of the town. We shared a brief hug, and she told me she was sorry. When we parted ways, she told me to take care of myself. She didn't call me handsome—the way she'd always done before.

The thing was, I wasn't that damn sad about it. She wasn't the one for me anyway. Somewhere—deep inside—I'd always known that.

Dad wouldn't want me to spend my time on the island mourning him, so I didn't know what I was really doing there, then—not until the sun started coming up over the clear water, anyway.

"Hello, beautiful," I whispered. "Look at you." The colors looked the same as they did at the ranch, only they added their beauty to the sparkling water instead of the snow-capped mountains.

Slowly, the shadows over the water began to fill with the sun's light until not one shadow remained. Seabirds called out their good mornings to all who were awake at the early hour. Some fish splashed happily in the water.

I took in a deep breath of salty sea air. "Ah, this is nice. This alone is worth the trip."

Once the sun was all the way up, I went inside to see what kind of breakfast I could rustle up. The coffeemaker was some fancy thing, but I figured it out without even reading the directions. There were eggs and bacon in the fridge and a loaf of wheat bread in the bread box.

Breaking out the frying pan, I went to work making my first meal on the island. Soon, I found the smell of bacon paired just as good with salty sea air as it did with cool mountain air. "Ah."

After eating breakfast, I set to work unpacking my bags and putting everything away. Then I showered, shaved, and put on a fresh pair of starched blue jeans, a white, long-sleeve, pearl-snap button-down, my tan Lucchese boots I'd bought especially for the island, and a brand new Stetson cowboy hat. Looking in the mirror, I commented, "Not bad, Pitt Zycan. Not bad at all."

The phone in the living area rang, and I went to answer it. "Pitt here."

"I know," Galen said. "We're heading to breakfast. Should I come to get you? Or do you think you can find your way to The Royal? It's straight up the pathway and easy to find."

"I've already had my breakfast, thank you very much." I knew I would most likely always be ahead of the man when it came to meal time. "How about I catch you for lunch around eleven?"

"Um—no." He laughed. "Maybe we can meet for dinner. How's nine-thirty for you?"

"It's not a great time for eating as I'll likely have been asleep for about a half hour by that time. Early to bed and early to rise, you know." I had no idea just how off our schedules would be.

"You don't have animals to care for here, Pitt." He chuckled. "I tell you what. We can meet for drinks at one of the bars here. How about at Cantina Cordova at noon? You just leave your bungalow and go to the right, then come along the beach to a large open-air hut with a bar in the middle of it. You can't miss it."

"I'll be there with bells on, Galen. See you then." I hung up the phone and went to check out the television, only to find there wasn't one. "Well, what the hell am I supposed to do with my time off now?"

It was ten in the morning. No television to entertain me. But there was a beach to walk down. And a bar to go to, apparently.

Taking off, I walked out of the bungalow to find a group of people hardly moving around. All of them wore dark sunglasses, shorts, and short-sleeved shirts with flip-flops. I walked along the beach, making sure to keep my boots out of the waves that lapped along the shoreline.

Well, let's see what today brings my way.

CHAPTER 4

Kaylee

S etting up the bar at ten in the morning might've sounded crazy at most places, but Paradise Resort wasn't like most places. Shortly after breakfast many of the guests began to take walks, and most of them added a cocktail or two to their excursions.

"Mornin', ma'am," came a deep, masculine voice from behind me as I reached up to place a bottle of Blue Curacao on the top shelf.

I turned to greet my very first guest of the day. "Good morning." I turned around and paused, not expecting to find a handsome cowboy standing at the bar. "Sir."

I'd been working on the island for a couple of weeks and had yet to see a cowboy. Or anyone wearing blue jeans and cowboy boots. Or a long sleeve shirt. Or a cowboy hat.

"Ya' think you can make me up something exotic and not make it too strong?" He took a seat on the barstool closest to me. "It's early for drinkin', but with no television, I'm not sure what else to do."

Thick, dark curls hung to his earlobes and the bluest eyes I'd ever seen shone at me as he smiled, revealing white, straight teeth. "I can rustle up something for you," I mimicked his southern drawl before thinking better about doing that. *My sassy ways might get my butt fired.* "Sorry about that. It's a bad habit I picked up from working at a bar in Austin, Texas. We would joke around with the guests there. But that bar had quite a different atmosphere than here at the resort."

"I don't mind." He tapped one thick, long finger on the wooden bar top. "How 'bout something blue and coconutty?"

Pulling my eyes away from his proved to be a challenge, but I managed. "I can do that for you, sir."

"Sir?" he chuckled, making his broad chest and shoulders shake. "I'm Pitt. Just Pitt. 'Kay?"

"Of course." I pointed to my nametag. "And I'm Kaylee. It's nice to meet you, Pitt." I got to work on his drink, making sure to keep the alcohol to a minimum per his request.

"So, what kinds of things are there to do on this island, Kaylee?" he asked me.

I bit my lower lip, resisting the temptation to make a smart remark about there not being any cattle to herd or horses who needed breaking.

Down, girl!

"Did I hear you say something about the television?" I asked, instead of making a crack that might not go over well with this man I didn't even know.

"I did." He watched me intensely as I made his drink. "There's not one in my cabin. I mean, bungalow."

"You know, all you've got to do is tell your hostess that you'd like one, and she'll get that done for you ASAP?" I put a small napkin down, then placed the tall skinny glass on it. "Here you are. It's kind of like a Blue Hawaiian—only better. I've named it the Paradise Blues. Tell me what you think, Pitt."

He took a sip then smiled at me. "I think it tastes like paradise. Very nice, Kaylee." He put the drink back down, then looked out at the water. "Sure is pretty out here. I could watch the water from my deck all day. As far as the hostess goes, I told Galen not to bother with that."

I couldn't believe it. *Someone here* didn't *want to be catered to?*

"You told him *not* to set you up with a hostess?" Maybe he preferred a man to do his bidding. "You know, he can set you up with a host if you'd like. You know, a guy instead of a girl?"

He shook his head, making his curls bounce a little. I found the movement surprisingly sexy.

Whoa, what?

I was certainly not used to looking at my customers and having thoughts like that.

"Hell, I don't need no one waitin' on me." He took another drink. "Shoot, this really is good, girl."

I wasn't sure how to approach the subject or if I even should, but I went and asked anyway. "You don't have people at your home to take care of things for you?"

Leaning back, he stretched his long legs out, and I couldn't help but notice how muscular they were under his tight blue Wrangler jeans. Nor could I help but notice the way my insides got all hot.

"Well, we got Cookie, I guess." He looked off in the distance. "He cooks. And Mom has Stella, who helps her clean the house. It's way too big for her to clean it all on her own. And there are a few ranch hands who help out, too. But we don't have anyone cater to any of us. Not Grandpa, not Mom, me, or my three sisters. Although, I bet if my sister Lucy could get away with having a servant, she would most definitely do that."

I was starting to put a picture together about this ruggedly handsome man. "So, you come from a big family, then?"

"I do." He picked up the glass and took another drink. "My mother's father started the Pipe Creek Ranch over fifty years ago. We live on it and work it still. It's outside of Gunnison, Colorado. Two-thousand acres and a bunch of cattle, chickens, dogs, cats, and my family."

I'd never heard of a rancher being a billionaire. I knew only the wealthiest individuals on the planet were invited to Mr. Dunne's resort, and I didn't imagine the man in front of me would be an exception—regardless of how different he was from the rest of the guests I'd met. I also knew it was none of my business, but I asked anyway. "So, how did you manage to make enough money to be invited here, Pitt?"

"Oh," he nodded. "That'd be from my dad." He looked at me with those crazy hot blue eyes, and I found his lips tilting down at the corners. "He passed away a little over a year ago. Damned cigarettes gave him lung cancer. Please tell me you don't smoke, Kaylee."

"I don't smoke. And I'm sorry to hear about your father." I couldn't help the smile that crept over my lips. "Thanks for caring."

He nodded his head, then took another drink before going on. "Dad and Galen were business partners. My father helped him invent a marine engine that Galen later sold to the military. It made them billions. The military spends way more than most any other private company in the world. Galen knew that, but he had to convince my father that they were the ideal customer. Boy, did those two argue. But Dad had to eat his words when Galen showed him how much money they'd made when he went with his idea."

"I bet." I couldn't believe the family still worked the ranch themselves with all the money they now had. "So, why keep the ranch? Isn't it hard work? Or do you guys just get someone else to do all the hard work?"

"Hell, no!" He slammed his hand down playfully on the bar. "We still do all that work. It's hard, yes. But man, it's worth it." That charming smile pulled his lips up again, and I felt my knees going weak.

Stop it!

I stood up nice and tall, trying not to let the handsome man get to me. He was rich and a bit older than I was—around thirty, I thought. He had to know his way around a woman. He'd chew me up and spit me out if I let him.

"So, you're telling me that you get up before dawn and work cattle and stuff like that?" I asked, because I just couldn't believe a man with so much money would do a thing like that.

He nodded. "I get up at four every morning, and I take a four-wheeler from our house up to the barn behind my grandpa's house. From there, I pick out a horse to spend the day with. We go out to whatever pasture the cattle were left in the night before and start moving them to another pasture."

"And why do you bother these cows so early in the morning?" I had to ask. "And why make them move to another pasture at all?"

He laughed. "We do it so early because there's a shit-ton more to do each day. And we move them from one pasture to another to give the grass a chance to grow." Picking up his drink, he nodded at me. "I like the questions you ask, Kaylee." He took a sip, then put the glass back down. "I bet you're pretty smart about lots of things, aren't ya'?"

"I like to think so." I picked up a bar towel to wipe glasses down. "I never thought I'd be a bartender forever, but I think I've found my career here at this resort. Being a bartender back in Austin didn't cut it for me, but here? I think it will work out just fine, living and working in paradise. Plus, the people I wait on are much nicer. Not as crass as a lot of the people I waited on back home."

He laughed, and the sound filled the air. "I bet you had to beat the boys off with a stick."

"Yeah, sometimes." I felt a little uneasy talking to him about that, and I felt my cheeks heat a little. "Anyway, if you don't want to get a hostess or anyone like that bothering you, I can make sure you get a television taken to your bungalow."

The way his jaw hung open as he looked at me made my heart skip a beat. "You'd do that for me?"

"Sure," I said as I smiled at him. "Why wouldn't I?"

"Oh, yeah." He picked up his drink, draining it before placing it on the bar. "You're here to please, right?"

"Yes, I am." He made it seem like it was a Herculean task. It might not be part of my job as a bartender, exactly, but I'd hardly be going out of my way. "Besides, you seem like a hardworking man who deserves a break. Plus, you're a rancher. I love steak. You make steaks possible."

"Yeah, I do." He braced his arm on the bar as he leaned in closer to me. "Kaylee, what do you think about joining me for dinner later on this evening? I would imagine that since you're working right now, you won't be by then. You're a nice girl. You're an interesting girl. It would be my pleasure to get to know you better."

Is he hitting on me? I couldn't believe it.

My jaw got tight, disappointed that he had more in common with the clientele at my old job than I'd first assumed. And then my mouth got smart, too. "Look, I know what you're looking for, and I'm not that kind of girl, Pitt. I'm not into hook ups. I'm not into being someone's companion for a few months then having them leave me at the end of their vacation, either. I will not be used in any way. I'm holding out for something more."

His eyes went wide, then after a brief moment, his lips turned up slightly in a smile. "Like what, Kaylee?"

I didn't owe him any answers. I didn't have to say another word to the man. No one would've expected me to explain myself if I didn't want to. I'd been through a sexual harassment training program when I first got to the island. We could date anyone we wanted to, and we could turn down dates when we wanted to as well. We weren't allowed to do anything for money or gifts, ever. And we didn't have to explain a thing to our guests.

But I opened my mouth anyway. "I'm holding out for true love."

CHAPTER 5

Pitt

Golden-brown eyes darted away from mine as I processed the words the beautiful bartender had just spoken. I'd already been impressed with her, but that sentence really blew me away.

Her dark, curly hair was held together in a long braid, which swung over her shoulder as she turned away from me quickly. I watched as she started rearranging the bottles of alcohol behind the bar, clearly trying to put an end our conversation.

The way her flowery tank top fit her perfectly, accenting her perky, plump tits made my mouth water. She also had one of the nicest asses I'd ever seen, and it bounced a little as she stepped along the bar, moving around more bottles. She was round in all the right places, and I bet she knew that, too.

It was apparent that she didn't want to talk to me about a dinner date, but I had to know more about her answer. "Hell, girl. I wasn't asking you to be my soulmate. It's just dinner and maybe some drinks. How will you ever find true love if you refuse to get to know anyone over a few drinks?"

I liked the way her lower lip was plumper than her upper one. And I also liked the way she pulled it between her straight, white teeth as she turned around to face me. "I haven't quite worked that out yet. And I'm quite aware that you weren't asking me to be your soulmate."

Shaking my head, I couldn't believe that this girl who'd just given such a straightforward answer hadn't thought out some plan for how she was going to find the true love she spoke of. "If you don't mind me sayin' so, I think your plan of waiting for true love might have some flaws. It might even be a bit naïve. About how old are ya', anyway?"

"I'm twenty-two," she snapped. "And I'm not naïve. I'm overly jaded, if you must know—much more so than most people my age. I just know that I don't want a long list of names when I think about all the men I've kissed."

The girl had her own standards, and she stuck to them. I liked that. "How long's that list right now, Kaylee?"

A wry smile curled her lips. The girl wore her makeup beautifully, using just enough to highlight her natural beauty and creamy tanned skin. "That list is none of your business, Pitt."

"That short then," I said with a crooked smile. Tipping my hat to her, I added, "Ain't nothin' wrong with that."

Her chest rose and fell as she took a deep breath. "There's no list."

I had to let that sink in a bit. "No list? Like, you've never kissed a man? Like, ever?" The thought that this gorgeous young woman had never been kissed just didn't sit right with me.

"No, I've never been kissed." She crossed her arms, resting them just underneath her bountiful breasts. "And I don't plan on kissing some man I hardly know after one date. Isn't that what's expected? One date equals at least one kiss. Right?"

"It doesn't have to. Though that's the way it goes a lot of the time, I'll give you that." I thought about taking her to dinner that night, then walking her back to her place. Standing at her door, then leaning in and taking those plump, juicy lips of hers with a sweet kiss.

A kiss that would go from sweet to passionate. And then she might invite me in for a much-needed roll in the hay.

I shook my head. She had just told me in no uncertain terms that that was one fantasy that would *not* be happening.

"See, that's what you would expect if I accepted your offer." She put her hand on her round hip, jutting it out a little. The way the khaki shorts moved up one leg a bit gave me a nice view of her toned upper thigh. "And then I'd always remember you as my first kiss. And what if we didn't hit it off? What if we didn't mesh well? You're a cowboy. I'm a bartender from a big city. We part ways, and there I am, left with the first guy on a list I never wanted to have. I want one man —just one—on that list."

My cock thumped as another realization struck. "So, you're a twenty-two-year-old virgin."

She nodded. "And I'm not looking to change that any time soon. So don't ask if you can help me out with that."

All I could do was shake my head. "I'm not like that." But I was curious about why she'd held onto that asset longer than most. "You religious or something like that?"

"Not really. I'm not keeping my virginity for anyone but myself." She looked down as a blush covered her cheeks. "And for a man I can be sure of—the one I'll know will be the only man I'll ever love."

She had the right idea, if you asked me, but was going about it the wrong way. "Honey, how are you ever going to find this one man if you never go out with anyone? How will you know who he is if you never kiss a few men to find out which one stirs you the way you must think will happen when you find the one for you?"

"Let me ask you a question, Pitt," she said as she leaned on the bar a few feet down from where I sat. "I'm sure you've had more than a few girls in your time. What are you, about thirty?"

"Thirty-two." I figured I could educate the girl a bit. "And I lost my virginity when I was seventeen to a twenty-year-old college girl who I never saw again. I played the field for a few years—and no, I didn't keep a list of who I had sex with. I dated a couple of girls briefly before dating one for years, but nothing came of that. And here's the thing, honey, I don't regret any of it. Not a bit."

"Yeah, most people don't," she said, nodding. "But I'm not most people. And you might not keep a list of all the women you've had sex with, but I bet you have a mental one. I bet you've—at the very least—got a number of how many different girls you've slept with. And I bet you're even pretty proud of your accomplishments. Am I wrong?"

A small part of me wished she were wrong. "Nope." That girl didn't know the first thing about sex. "Wouldn't it be worse if I didn't remember the women I'd been with? Of course I remember them. Having different partners can teach you many different things about intimacy, not the least of which is how to perfect your lovemaking techniques. I could even fill you in on some of them if you'd like," I teased her a little; I couldn't help myself.

"No interested," she snipped as she went back to moving bottles around, trying to look busy.

"Talking about sex makes you nervous," I pointed out. "It doesn't have to, honey—it's a natural part of life."

When she turned back around, I found her chewing her lower lip and looking a little peeved. "Okay, Pitt. My name is Kaylee, not Honey. And of course talking about something so intimate with a total stranger makes me nervous. And quite frankly, I would love nothing more than to get off this subject. How about we talk about what kinds of television shows you like to watch? Or we can talk about how blue the sky is today. Or we can even talk about how your trip getting to the island was. All of those things are what I normally talk about with people I don't know."

"You're about as easy to get to know as a cactus, aren't you?" I had to ask. "Do you mind me askin' how many close friends you have?"

Her new chore of wiping the bar down with a dishcloth had her putting in some elbow grease, although there wasn't a spot on the pristine surface. "I do mind you asking that, actually. How would you like it if I asked you something that personal?"

"I've got five close friends." I had no problem talking to her about that. And then I sat back and realized something incredible.

I have no problem talking to her about anything.

Now my grandpa was a man of few words. And I do mean few. He never said hello when anyone came through his door. Sometimes he'd say leave. Sometimes he'd say go away. But I could not recall ever hearing that man say hello. Not to anyone.

Almost every woman I'd ever had a romantic relationship with had told me that I didn't talk enough. They accused me of not trying to get to know them or of not caring about them. And I had to admit that was partially the truth. No one had ever inspired me to want to get to know them.

So what the hell am I doing with this girl?

Kaylee's tone took on a sarcastic note as she said, "Good for you, Pitt. You've got five close friends. And here I thought real working cowboys didn't have time to make friends."

"We don't." I stood and leaned on the bar, looking her over. "They're all from childhood. Back from before I had to work from sunup to sundown. But I still consider them close friends, even though years go by without us talking or seeing each other. When it comes down to it, if I need them, they're there. That means a lot to me. And something's botherin' me about you, Kaylee." I drummed my fingers on the bar. "It bothers me that you don't have any close friends."

"I didn't say that I didn't have any close friends. I said that I didn't want to answer the question. I'd rather not talk about my personal life with a stranger." She huffed, then picked up the empty glass I'd left on the bar. "You want another one?"

"I want you to come to dinner with me." I looked at her and gave her my most intense stare. It worked on defiant horses and cattle; I hoped it might work on her, too.

"Well, some people don't always get what they want." She smiled an actual smile that told me she was so proud of herself for sticking to her *no.*

I didn't know what the hell I was doing. The girl was stuck-up, high on the success of keeping her virginity locked up tight. Her snarkiness told me she was also most likely a real bitch when she didn't get things her way.

Maybe she wasn't worth my time after all. Why should I spend my time trying to date someone who clearly had all her walls up—and then some?

I turned to leave, but before I walked away I couldn't resist getting a little swipe in. "No wonder you don't have any friends, Kaylee." And then I let my boots take me away from the beautiful young woman who'd gotten more words out of me than any who'd come before her.

The island was full of gorgeous women. I was sure of that. So what if Kaylee didn't want to eat dinner with me? I didn't come to the island to hook up, anyway.

I just kept walking without looking back. All I knew for sure was that I would not be going back to that bar again. I would not set my eyes upon her, not after knowing how determined she was to be lonely.

Who wants to be that lonely?

I'd sat in the saddle most of my life, watching cattle graze, all alone. But I wasn't opposed to being with people the way Kaylee was. I wasn't opposed to getting to know someone—even if I hadn't yet found anyone that I thought was truly worth the knowing.

One thing was for sure, though. I'd spent enough time alone in my life to know that that girl would never find love if she kept herself apart like that forever.

CHAPTER 6

Kaylee

"**M**an, his ass does look great in those jeans," I sighed and muttered to myself as I watched Pitt leave my bar.

Being a bartender in Austin, I'd seen tons of great asses in tight blue jeans. Pitt's was the best though—hands down.

Ranching was clearly a great way to stay fit, because his body was in perfect shape. Despite the way the conversation had ended between us, I couldn't help but wonder what he'd look like naked and sprawled out on a bed somewhere. Maybe he'd gaze at me with those deep blue eyes. Maybe he'd have an erection that would be so big it would scare me.

I shook my head and looked away from the man as he walked back up the beach. *Why am I thinking this way?*

It wasn't like I was a saint. I had seen nice-looking men before. But Pitt was better looking than any man I'd ever seen in real life. He had this unique quality to him that I couldn't exactly pinpoint.

And I'd just blown him off the same way I blew everyone off. He'd hit the nail on the head, though. He was right; I had no close friends.

I had acquaintances. I had coworkers. But I had no close friends. And there was nobody to blame but me for that.

People began to filter into the bar, and I had to get to work and get my mind off my own personal issues. "Hi, Mr. and Mrs. Jamison! What can I get for you today?"

"A couple of gin and tonics," Mrs. Jamison ordered. "How's the water today, Kaylee?"

"The water was nice and warm when I dipped my toes in before getting to work this morning." I made their simple drinks, then placed them on the bar. "Did you two have a nice breakfast this morning?"

Mrs. Jamison smiled as she picked up her drink. "I had French toast. It was delicious." She looped her arm through her husband's. "We're going to go sit on the sand and enjoy the warm sunshine. Thanks for the drinks."

The couple left, and I watched as they strolled away, talking to each other quietly. Mrs. Jamison's husband held her hand while she took a seat on the sandy beach, then she took his drink, holding it for him while he took a seat next to her. They kissed as she handed him the drink, then he put his arm around her shoulders, and she rested her head on his.

"Sweet," I whispered.

I began to wonder if they had always known that they were meant to be together.

Deep inside me, doubt began to form. For the first time in my life, I'd started to question whether the way I'd been living was really working for me.

Pitt was right, it would be very hard to find the one man I was sure was out there for me if I never dated. But what if I ended up giving my first kiss away to the wrong man?

Maybe Pitt would be a gentleman and respect my wishes, not pressuring me for a kiss at the end of a date. He did know about what I wanted, after all.

What harm could it do, going out with the man?

He did seem pretty ticked at me when he left, though. And he'd dropped that nasty little comment as he'd walked away. He might even turn me down if I went to him with an apology and told him I'd decided to accept his offer of dinner.

His offer may be off the table now.

I didn't have to go to him and tell him any of that. I could go to him with my own offer. Maybe that would help him to forgive me for my abrupt rejection. At the very least, I would know that I'd tried.

For the first time ever, I felt like I actually wanted to try to get to know a man. And I would try to let him get to know me. The real me, not the girl I hid from almost everyone.

He might not even like the real me. But then again, he just might. It really could go either way, because I was kind of a dork without my guard up.

My mind went straight to planning, figuring out what I was going to do when my shift was over. And by the time my coworker Tony showed up to relieve me, I had my plan set out.

Hurrying to my room, I changed into white shorts, some cute sandals, and a pink top that I tied at the waist. I pulled my hair out of its braid and gave my naturally curly hair a spritz from a water bottle before running some leave-in conditioner through it with my fingers. It smelled like coconut and lime and hung down my back in shiny curls. I felt cute, and I usually never felt cute.

Heading to the kitchen, I found a takeout bag and got to work making a picnic for us to share. In the fridge, I found cheese, some white wine, and some thinly sliced meats that I put on a tray then covered with plastic wrap. Adding a couple of wine glasses and a tablecloth I found in a drawer, I grabbed all my supplies then headed out to find Pitt. I hoped he hadn't found anyone else to go to dinner with. But it was only five, so I had high hopes I'd get to him before he set out.

I'd seen Mr. Dunne at the bar earlier and asked him which bungalow Pitt was staying in. I didn't give him any details of our encounter, but told him that I wanted to make sure Pitt got a television delivered. I'd called Camilla to get that done before I left the bar.

As I expected, I heard the television going as I walked up to his door. My stomach was a mess of butterflies, and I knew I had every right to feel nervous.

Clenching my fist, I lifted it and knocked three times. "Please don't let him slam the door in my face," I muttered to myself.

"Come on in," he drawled from just inside the door as he pulled it open. But then he saw that it was me standing there. "What do you want?"

Yep, still pissed at me.

I held up the bag in my hand. "I'm sorry. I've brought a peace offering. I'm going to take this picnic I made with you in mind and have a little dinner on the beach. I was wondering if you wanted to share it with me. Did I mention that I'm sorry?"

"You did." He took a deep breath as he looked at me. "And what made you decide to come here with your peace offering?"

I shrugged because I wasn't sure. "I don't know, Pitt. I just know that I didn't like you walking away from me. And I didn't like how I felt as I watched you leave. So all day I've been thinking about how I could apologize and try to become your friend, and this is what I came up with. A picnic on the beach." I shook the bag. "There's wine in here, too."

Finally, a smile moved his lips, and it went all the way up to his eyes. "I've got beer in here." He jerked his head toward the kitchen. "Come on in." He took a step back so I could walk inside.

"I hear the television has arrived," I commented as I put the bag on the countertop.

"Yep. I suppose I have you to thank for that." He pulled open the fridge then got out two beers. Popping the top off one, he walked over, handing it to me. "Please tell me that you drink beer, Kaylee."

I took it from him, taking a nice long drink. "Ah. I do drink beer, Pitt."

"Wine is fine, but beer is life." He walked to the living room and took a seat on the sofa. "Come on in here and take a seat. After this beer, we can go outside and drink that wine and eat the dinner you've made for us."

Taking my beer, I went to sit on the other end of the sofa. "Okay." I tapped my fingers on the cool glass bottle. I didn't know what to say.

"You like football?" he asked as he looked at me out of the corner of his eye.

"Um, well, I've watched tons of games. Working at a bar, you can imagine how busy we get when games are on." I took a sip of my drink before going on. "Truth is, I can't say I have any one team I root for or root against. But I find the game exciting."

"Cool." He took a drink then smiled. "I like the Broncos."

"Hey, they won the Superbowl recently, didn't they?" I sort of remembered people cheering them on one year not too long ago.

"They did." He turned his head to look at me. "So, you feel like making them your favorite football team, Kaylee?"

"Why not?" I took another drink. "You know what, I've never drank with a patron of any of the bars I've worked at before."

"I'm glad to be your first then." He raised his bottle and winked. "Here's to hanging out together."

I nodded and thought that sounded pretty cool. I tapped his bottle with mine. "To hanging out." We each took a sip of our drinks, and I liked the way it made me feel. Like we were really doing something together. Really, I just liked the way he made me feel. "You're alright, Pitt."

"I know." He smiled, then got up and walked over to turn off the television. "They forgot to bring the remote, I think."

I got up and headed to the phone. "Well, that's not okay at all." I looked over my shoulder at him. "Did you want a television in your bedroom, too?"

"Man, I like you." He said with a smile. "That would be awesome."

"Right?" I laughed as I called Camilla. "Hi, Mrs. Chambers. Mr. Zycan did receive the television, but they forgot the remote. And he's going to need another set for his bedroom, too. Can you send someone out to make that happen? And please remind them not to forget the remotes."

She assured me that it would be taken care of right away, and I hung up and walked toward the kitchen. "Would you like to go out and get this picnic started? I know it's early, but I'm starving. I haven't eaten since breakfast."

"Actually, this is perfect. I always eat around five when I'm home." He walked past me as I picked up the bag. "I'm usually in bed by nine."

I laughed. "When I was working in Austin, I never got to bed before three or four each morning. Since I've been here, working the day shift, I've gone to bed at nine every single night and have loved it. I couldn't tell you the last time I saw the sunrise back in Austin. But here, I've made sure to wake up to catch it every morning."

He gazed at me for a moment. "Watching the sunrise is one of my favorite things to do. I actually enjoy them more than sunsets."

As we headed to the beach, I felt I needed to let him know why I'd been so defensive with him earlier at the bar. I was glad he'd accepted my peace offering, but I still like I had some explaining to do—not for his sake, so much as mine.

"Pitt, I've been thinking all day about what you were saying to me earlier, and I think you were right in a lot of ways. I've built up this wall to protect myself from men who only want to use me. I know it's not right to treat each man as if that's all he wants, but at a certain point, it became easier than getting my hopes up again and again.

"I can't make any promises about how good I'll be at it, but I feel like opening up to you a bit is something I'd like to try. I don't normally do this with anyone, not just my customers. It's not necessarily natural to me."

"I know it's not." He took a step away from me, putting a little more distance between us. "And I won't take this lightly, Kaylee. I promise."

CHAPTER 7

Pitt

I had to hand it to the girl; she knew how to make an apology.

Working together, we spread out the tablecloth she'd brought, then sat down. "I like picnics," I let her know. "It's not something I get to do very often. Like, not since I was a kid. But I do like them."

"I thought you might." Kaylee poured the wine then handed me a glass. "I know it's not beer, but it's good for the heart. Or so I hear, anyway. Plus, it goes well with the cheese and meats."

I looked at the tiny foods she'd prepared and couldn't help but chuckle. "Yeah, this will make a great snack."

She looked at the offering and laughed. "Yeah, I didn't really think this out very well, did I?"

"It's the thought that counts." I picked up a tiny cheese wedge and ate it. "I'll cook us some steaks on the pit out on the deck later. There are some real good-looking ones in the fridge in my cabin—I mean, bungalow."

She smiled at me. Not that snarky smile she'd done back at the bar when she was telling me off. No, this smile was real. "I would offer to help out with cooking, but I kind of suck at it."

"You know, where I come from, girls use their cooking skills to bag a husband." I liked the fact that she wasn't trying to do that with me. Hell, she wasn't trying to do that with anyone.

"Maybe that's why I've never cared much about learning how, then." She laughed and dropped her head back. Her long hair blew around her pretty face as she let loose a little. "I like this."

"Me, too." I could tell that she was feeling more comfortable around me. "You're pretty easy to hang out with, Kaylee. I bet you're full of surprises, too."

"Oh, I don't know." She took a drink of wine then picked up a piece of ham. "I'm kind of boring."

"I doubt that very much." I would've bet a million bucks that the girl wasn't nearly as boring as she thought she was.

She shook her head. "No, Pitt. I really am boring. I don't know if it comes from working in a fast-paced, exciting atmosphere or what, but my idea of what is a good time just isn't what most people my age think."

"Hit me with one of the things you do for fun, then." I leaned back on my hands, stretched out my legs and looked at her, giving her my full attention.

She sat up, crossing her long legs and said, "Okay, I like to veg out on my bed, binge watch old shows like *I Love Lucy*, and munch on peanut butter and grape jelly sandwiches while throwing back a glass of milk."

"What's wrong with that?" I asked. "Sounds like fun to me. You've got good food, a great drink, and you're watching some funny shit. What's not to like about that?"

She shrugged. "No one I ever knew thought it was fun. Everyone says I'm boring." She looked at me with a certain amount of intensity. "Okay, I'm going to give you another example of what I find fun. Now, I don't want you to tell me what you think I want to hear. I want you to be honest. Promise me."

"I promise I'll be honest." And then I thought I should be honest about myself, too. "I'm kind of too honest at times."

"'Kay." She nodded, bracing herself like she was about to make some huge confession. "When I got here to the island, I found this tree on the interior part. It's huge and must be really old. I found some scrap wood and some nails and a hammer. On my days off, which I've only had a few of so far, I've been building a treehouse. I haven't told anyone because I'm sure they'd think I'm crazy—who builds a tree house on an island resort?"

I couldn't help but grin. "Show it to me."

"Really?" she asked.

"Really." I got up, then held out my hand for her to take. "I've got to see this."

"Okay, come on then." She pulled her hand out of mine—I'd guessed she would—then we gathered up our things. "We can finish our picnic in what I've built so far. It's nowhere near finished. It may never be finished. But the view is so beautiful."

"Back home, I've got this one barn that my grandpa stopped using because it leaked too bad." I took the bag from her so I could carry it. "I've been using those leaks to make waterfalls. Every time it rains, I head out to that barn to see how things look and I always find myself making little adjustments to make the water fall a little bit differently. I love that old barn."

"That sounds cool—beautiful, too." She laughed as she took a right off the pathway. "It's through here."

"You weren't afraid to go through this jungle alone, Kaylee?" I asked, thinking that most of the women I knew wouldn't have taken one step off the path.

"Why would I be?" She looked back at me as she led the way. "Being a loner isn't always a bad thing. I've learned how to do a lot of things on my own, I guess."

"I bet you have." We rounded a bend and there it was. "Whoa!"

It wasn't exactly spectacular, but it was getting there. And she was well aware of that.

"So far, I've found enough wood to make the floor, the steps up the tree, and that's about it. But wait 'til you see the view from up there." She looked at my boots, then up my body. "Can you climb in what you're wearing?"

"Hell yes I can." She had no idea who she was hanging with. "Get on up that tree. I'm right behind ya'."

She climbed up, and I tried not to look at the fantastic view of her ass that was provided for me.

Be a gentleman, Pitt.

Climbing up and joining her on the floor of her treehouse, I saw exactly why she would want to build a tree house here. "We're above it all."

"Yeah, it's great, huh?" she said, looking at me then down at the bag I'd left on the ground. "You forgot our picnic."

"That ain't much of a loss, now is it?" I laughed and ran my arm around her shoulders. "This is cool up here. What in the hell made you decide to climb this tree?"

She shrugged, but didn't seem to be worried about my arm being around her. I liked that. "The tree was big. It looked sturdy. So I climbed it. I always loved climbing things when I was younger; my mother actually used to call me Monkey." Her brow furrowed. "I was diagnosed with ADHD when I was sixteen. My parents thought it best to put me on meds for it. I hated how they made me feel, and when I turned eighteen, I stopped taking the meds.

"I made it my mission to stop acting so hyper. It wasn't that hard to do, really. I just stopped all the moving around so much—at least, when I was around people. When my mind wanders, I find some-thing to focus on until I've got it back under control. Not that I always have it under control. But I try. And I shut up a lot, too, when I feel it getting out of my hands."

"I see." I knew she was really putting herself out there—opening up, just like she said she was going to. "How many people know this about you, Kaylee?"

"Only four or five. Mom and Dad know, obviously. The principal of my high school and one or two of the teachers there were told. I never told any of my college teachers or anyone at the bar in Austin. And no one here, either."

To say I felt special didn't cut it. But a change had come over her since she started talking about this; her head sank, like she was embarrassed. I couldn't have that.

I moved my arm off her shoulders and took her by the chin to make her look at me. "Hey, there's nothing wrong with you. You're great. Well, you can be great once you understand that it's perfectly okay to be who you are. I bet it's hard as hell to keep that all tamped down all the time. And all on your own, too. Not even taking any medication to help you. Shit. I'm impressed by how well you've done all on your own."

"You are?" she asked as she searched my eyes. "You're not just saying that?"

"Hell no." I knew then why she acted the way she did. She was trying to be someone she wasn't. "Look, I bet if you can learn that people will accept you the way you are, then you're going to start feeling a lot better about life and people in general. And I just happen to have the next few months free to help you learn how to do that."

She laughed. "Pitt, I don't think you've got any idea what you'd be getting into with me. I can be a real dork." She gestured to the tree-house. "As you can see by where I like to spend my free time. And if you knew what I want to do at the swimming pools instead of lying around on floats, letting the sun bake my skin, you'd shake your head in embarrassment."

"Try me." I moved my hand down to hold hers. "I'll be right there with you. I'm telling you, once you stop trying to live like someone you're not, things will change for you. Your coworkers will get to know you. You'll make real friends, Kaylee. I promise you that you will."

"You really think so?" she asked with a frown. "Because I don't think that's what'll happen at all, Pitt. I think everyone will know that I'm a big ol' weirdo and have been faking this persona this whole time."

"First of all, you haven't worked here that long. I asked Galen, and he said you just started a couple of weeks ago."

She smiled at me. "You asked Mr. Dunne about me?"

"I did. I found out all the dirt on you." I winked at her and squeezed her hand. "And what you need to know is that no one here really knows you yet anyway. They can't have any preconceived notions about who you are or what your personality is yet. You can show them who you are. And I'm gonna tell you right now that you sound like a hell of a lot of fun."

"Pitt, I swear to God if you're just telling me all of this to get into my pants, then I will kill you." She smacked me in the arm to prove she meant it.

All I could do was smile at her and tell her the God's honest truth. "Honey, if I want in your pants, I'll get there. Right now, I just want to be your friend."

"You do?" she asked me like she couldn't believe it. "I'd love to believe you."

"You can." I inched forward, acting as if I was going to kiss her. And the fact she stayed perfectly still told me she was scared to death. When my lips touched her cheek instead of her lips, her body sagged with what I knew was relief. "Right now, I just want to be your friend, Kaylee Simpson."

CHAPTER 8

Kaylee

When I Pitt lowered his head to kiss me, I'd panicked. Thinking he was going to kiss my lips, my body froze, but I didn't stop him.

"Right now, I just want to be your friend, Kaylee Simpson."

My body released all the tension that had mounted in it when his lips pressed against my cheek. "Good," I sighed. I wasn't ready for anything more than that. "I see you also asked Mr. Dunne what my last name was. Did he give you my social security number, too?"

"Nope, just your last name." His blue eyes danced as he pulled his head back and looked into my eyes. "Would you like to go back to my place now? We can get to cookin' those steaks I told you about."

I nodded, then started climbing down the tree, but I didn't use the steps I'd nailed to the tree trunk. Grabbing a branch, I swung from it, then landed on another tree branch and made it down to the lowest branch before jumping to the ground.

Looking up, I found Pitt with his mouth hanging open. "Shit, you are part monkey, aren't you?"

Laughing, I nodded as I picked up the picnic bag. "I think I just might be."

He climbed down the normal way, then we headed back to his place. "I can teach you how to cook if you want, Kaylee."

"Why would I want to learn to do that?" I asked him as I led the way back to the main path.

"Because everyone should know how to cook." I felt his hand on my shoulder, and he pulled me back to get in front of me. "I'm not letting anyone see me getting led out of this jungle by a girl." He took the bag out of my hand, carrying it.

"What?" I darted through the trees to get in front of him again. "You don't even know the way back."

"I do, too." He grabbed me by the waist with one hand, picking me up and tossing me effortlessly over his shoulder. "Watch."

Laughing and breathless, I relaxed, more comfortable with the manhandling than I expected I'd be. And with my face pretty much even with his ass, I really couldn't complain about the view. "Are you really such a caveman, Pitt?"

"I'm a man, honey, not a caveman." He put me back on my feet as soon as we made it out of the jungle and were back on the path. "Here ya' go." He looked at me for a moment. "I know you told me not to call you honey, but it's just the way I talk. Promise not to hate me for it?"

"I guess you can call me that if you can't help it." Now that we were actually getting to know each other, I actually liked it when he called me that. No one had ever called me anything sweet before.

I felt at ease with Pitt in a way I hadn't with anyone else before. Maybe it was because we'd already had an argument and made up, too. It seemed to take the edge off things. And being honest with him about my ADHD had felt good.

Maybe I really can be myself on this island.

Once we got to his bungalow, he grabbed a couple of beers, then led me out to the deck. "You take a seat right here, lean back on this lounge chair while I get the fire going. It's about twenty minutes to sunset, and we can watch it together."

"You can really tell what time the sun is going to set just by looking at it?" I asked.

"I can." He turned on the gas grill, shaking his head as he did so. "Man, gas doesn't cook the same as charcoal, but it'll have to do."

"So, you really do work on the ranch, huh?" I had a hard time believing that with all that money in his family, he would actually choose to work so hard.

He looked at me with a slack jaw. "You didn't believe me?"

Shaking my head, I said, "Not really."

Grabbing his beer, he took the seat on the other lounge chair next to mine. "I know this might be hard to believe, but even with the money my family has, it hasn't stopped any of us from doing what we grew up doing. It's like ranching is in our blood. It's a part of us all—except for my youngest sister Harper. She could care less if she ever saw that place again. But she's not some spoiled rich girl, either. She's into science and inventing things, the way our dad was."

"So you get up really early and do all that work because you want to?" I asked as I shook my head in disbelief. "You get up and get on a horse and sit on it all day long, watching cows eat, because you like doing it?"

"Honey, I don't just sit on a horse all day." He laughed, then took a drink of his beer. "There are mornings that I don't really want to get up, but I do it anyway. And most of those mornings I get to see something spectacular, things I wouldn't ever see if I laid in bed not doing a thing just because I have money in the bank."

"What kinds of things?" I wanted to understand the man. I'd never cared to understand anyone before.

"Well, this one morning I wasn't feeling it. I had to drag my ass out of bed to get going that day. It was springtime when we sometimes get terrible thunderstorms out of nowhere. On my way to the barn, I could see lightning in the distance and knew I had to hurry myself up."

"If it was going to rain, why would you go out at all?" I didn't understand people who kept working in a storm.

"We had six heifers that were due to calve any day." He took another drink as he looked off in the distance. "A lot of times when storms come up, the cows go into labor. We don't like our cows to give birth outside in the middle of a storm. We want our calves to be born in a safe environment. So, we needed to round up those six heifers and get them into the barn. I met the other ranch hands there. Once my sisters heard the sound of thunder, they got their asses on horses, too, then we all set out to find those cows."

"And it was probably dark still, huh?" I could picture them all in my head. "Do your sisters look like you, Pitt?"

"We all have the same hair, but our eyes are each a little different." He laughed. "Are you picturing this in your head, Kaylee?"

"I am." I looked down. "Is it weird of me that I have a very active imagination?"

He shook his head. "No, it's damn smart if you ask me."

"Thanks." He had a way of making me feel good about just being me.

"Anyway, we all split up so we could cover more ground. And what I came upon was quite a sight." He shook his head as if he could see it all in his head. "There was a loud crackling sound, and then I saw a tree burst into flames as lightning struck it. The flames were so big that the trees around it caught on fire, too."

"Oh, damn." I sat up, the story taking a turn I hadn't seen coming. "What did you do?"

"What could I do?" He turned to look at me. "All I could do was start moving all the cattle away from there. And that might sound easy, but it wasn't. They were all panicked from the lightning and the fire. My horse was getting bumped on all sides, and he was getting panicky as well."

"Damn!" I clutched my beer bottle. "Did you end up getting hurt?"

"Thankfully, no." He looked up at the sky. "I think Dad was looking out for us. He'd only been gone a month when that happened. My horse took a kick to the ribs from a bull that was really losing his shit. He reared up, and I held on like my life depended on it. I'll admit I shouted, "Give me a break!" And then rain fell in sheets, putting out the fire and settling the herd. The cattle followed my horse and me up to the barn. Two of those mothers had their calves that morning. If I'd slept in, I would've missed all that."

I huffed. "You know, Pitt, I think most people would say that what you went through was terrible. You had to have been soaked to the bone, freezing cold."

"Yep." He took a drink. "But it was all worth it. I wouldn't have changed a single thing about that morning. Not one." He got up and went inside. "I'll grab those steaks. That grill ought to be hot enough by now."

I got up to follow him, thinking I should do something to contribute to the meal. "I can make a salad."

"What for?" Pitt took the steaks out of the fridge.

"You don't eat salad?" I asked, moving to stand on the other side of the bar.

"Do I look like a rabbit?" He walked outside with the steaks, shaking his head. "Toss a potato into the microwave for me instead."

"Okay." I should've known the man would have a strict diet of meat and potatoes. "What a caveman."

"I heard that," he called out to me from outside. "Hey, the sun's about to go down. Come on out here."

Walking back out, I stopped just outside the open glass doors. "It's pretty this evening. But then, it always is over the water."

Pitt closed the lid on the grill then came to stand next to me. He ran his arm around my shoulders. "This morning I watched my first sunrise on the island alone. And now I'm getting to watch my first sunset here with you. I've got to tell you, Kaylee, I much prefer sharing the experience with you."

I didn't know why I did it, but I leaned my head against his shoulder. "You know what? I've been watching these sunsets alone since I got here. And I've got to admit that this one seems a lot more colorful and bright than the others. Do you think that's just because I'm standing here with you, Pitt?"

His lips pressed against the top of my head. "I think so."

We stood there like that until the last colors left the sky. And then he let me go. I couldn't believe how quickly I missed his touch as he went to flip those steaks. "I better get that potato cooking for you."

My head felt light, and my heart felt heavy.

What are you doing, girl?

Pitt Zycan could not be *the* man. He and I weren't anywhere near the same league. Being a bartender from the city, I couldn't expect a billionaire rancher to fall in love with me.

And I wasn't giving up on my dreams of finding true love, not matter how tempting Pitt seemed. I knew I had to watch myself—keep my guard up at least a little bit. If I didn't, I knew I'd get hurt.

I'd managed to protect myself for a long time. Why would I go and put my heart on the line now?

"Hey, you want your steak rare, right?" he called from outside.

"Is there any other way?" I asked, his question pulling me out of my head.

"Not in my opinion, there's not." He came inside with the steaks on a plate. "You and I are a lot alike. You know that?"

"I think I'm starting to," I whispered to myself, hoping he wouldn't hear.

CHAPTER 9

Pitt

"I don't know how you eat that stuff." I shoveled a forkful of potato into my mouth.

She looked at her salad and shrugged. "It tastes good."

"Come on, that stuff doesn't have any flavor at all." I pointed to the bottle of ranch dressing that sat on the table near her. "That's what you taste right there. You like that ranch dressing, not the lettuce."

She stabbed a piece of lettuce that had no dressing at all. "Nope, I like the lettuce plain, too. See?"

She took the bite, and I wrinkled my nose as I thought about the flavor—or lack thereof. "Gross."

"Yum," she closed her eyes and moaned as if she really liked the stuff.

She sat with her back to the deck, so she couldn't see what I saw outside—lightning in the distance. A storm seemed to be heading our way. If it started raining, she would be stuck here for a while. And I thought that was a sign from above that I should make my move.

Sure, earlier I'd thought that just being her friend would be great, but she'd already grown on me. Plus, I felt like she was starting to trust me enough to forget about all that friend stuff and get right to the good stuff.

I picked up the TV remote and turned it on to drown out any sounds of thunder. "I hate to eat without any sound in the background. I hope you don't mind."

She shook her head, making her dark curls bounce around her pretty face. "I don't mind at all. I hate it when it's quiet and all you can hear is the sound of people chewing and gulping."

"Yeah, it's pretty gross." I watched as the lightning got closer and closer and then the rain began to fall.

Kaylee's head spun around as the sound of the rain became louder than the television. "Oh, crap!"

"What's the problem?" I asked, as if I didn't know.

"It's raining, and I've gotta walk back to my room is what's wrong." She bit her lower lip, looking worried.

"You don't have to get back there right now, do you?" I asked, getting up to put my empty plate away. "We can chill here and watch some television. No big deal."

She took the last bite of her steak then got up to clean her plate as well. "I'll do the dishes for you. You cooked; it's only fair that I clean up."

I wasn't going to argue. "Cool."

"And after that's done, I'll head out." She started filling the sink with soapy water, and I thought I must've heard her wrong.

"If the rain's finished." I went to take a seat on the sofa, taking the remote with me to find something we both might like to watch.

"I'm not waiting for the rain to stop. I can walk in the rain. I won't melt." She started washing the dishes, and I started thinking that she was scared to be alone with me, feeling trapped by the rain.

"It's not a big deal for you to hang out here until it stops, Kaylee. There's no need for you to rush out." I got up and went to get a bottle of water out of the fridge, then opened the freezer and saw some ice cream inside. "Plus, there's ice cream. We can let our meal settle, then have some dessert."

"I don't think that's a good idea." She looked over her shoulder, and I could swear I saw panic in her pretty golden-brown eyes.

Taking her by the chin, I drew her face back to look at me. "You don't have to be afraid of being here with me. You know that, right?"

She moved my hand off her face. "I know it seems silly, but I don't like not being able to leave when I want to." She got a hand towel out of a drawer, then dried the dishes.

"You shouldn't look at it like that." I took the dried plate out of her hand to put it back in the cabinet. "Mainly because you're not trapped. Just like you said, you can walk in the rain; you can leave whenever you want. No one's forcing you to stay, though I'd love it if you did."

Her chest heaved as she sighed heavily. "I guess you're right."

"I am right." I put away the rest of the dishes as she dried each one, then I took her hand and led her to the sofa. Sitting down next to her, I moved my arm to rest on the back of the sofa behind her. "You said you like watching funny shows, so I picked this one. If you don't like it, we can change it."

Her body felt rigid beside me, her back as straight as a board beside me. "This one is fine."

The damn rain seemed to really be bothering her. It didn't make a hell of a lot of sense to me. I draped my arm around her shoulders, pulling her closer to me. "Just relax, baby."

She turned her head to look at me. "Pitt, when you call me *honey*, it sounds like it just naturally flows out, like you call lots of people that. But, *baby* sounds like something a little different."

"You're right. I don't call everyone that." I smiled at her. "But it sounds right on you. I like you."

"Oh God." Somehow her body got even more rigid. "I knew this was a bad idea."

"This isn't a bad idea." I was losing her; I could tell by how wild her eyes went.

"This is too much like a date, Pitt." She pulled away from me, standing up. "This isn't hanging out. This isn't being friends. Do you think just because I haven't had many friends that I don't know that they don't put their arms around each other? They don't kiss on the cheek or anywhere else for that matter. They don't sit on the couch and snuggle while watching a movie either."

I ran my hand over my face in frustration. "Yeah, you're right." I pointed to the other end of the sofa. "Sit over there then. If that's what you want."

She shook her head. "I need to leave. I'm going to end up getting hurt if I don't." Then she walked toward the door.

I jumped up, not ready to let her go yet. "Kaylee, just stay. I'll chill. I'll keep my hands to myself if that's what you want. Just tell me so and I will. I promise."

She looked at me with fear in her pretty eyes. "Pitt, why do you like me? I mean, other than the fact that you're attracted to me physically?"

"And mentally," I told her.

"But you don't really know me." She sighed. "And I don't know you."

"Look, I'm simple. My friends call me a cowboy with a heart of gold." I laughed to lighten the mood. "And you're a bartender who's been hiding who she really is. You're much more interesting than any other guest here—people who've probably never worked a hard day in their life.

"I can help you while I'm here, and you can help me. We can help each other. No one is going to get hurt. You can trust me." I twirled a lock of her curly hair. "Look, we even have the same type of hair. We're just meant to be friends." I took off my hat and placed it on her head. "Plus, you look cute in my hat."

She reached out, moving her hand through my hair. "You should use the leave-in conditioner I do."

I moved her lock of hair up to my nose. "It smells too girly," I teased her. "Do they make any with manlier scents?"

"Probably." She stood there, gazing at me. "You're just about the most handsome man I've ever seen, Pitt. And that scares me."

"I've never been told that my looks scare anybody." I dragged my knuckles across her pink cheek. "And you're just about the prettiest girl I've ever seen. And I'm not one bit afraid of you." That wasn't entirely true. I was afraid that her skittishness would prevent her from ever giving me a real shot. And I wanted a real shot with her for some crazy reason.

Her eyes narrowed. "You just want my virginity."

"That's not all I want." I pulled her closer to me, wrapping my arms around her as I looked into her eyes. "That's part of the package —part of who you are—but it's not all I'm after. I thought I only wanted to be your friend, but it turns out I want more than that. But if friendship is all that's on the table, I don't want to miss out on that either."

She put her palm on my chest. "That's all I'm offering you right now—friendship. I'm not anywhere near ready to give up on my dream of finding true love."

"How do you know we can't find it together?" I ran my fingertip along her jawline.

She nodded as she continued to look me in the eyes. "I don't know that. What I do know is that I don't love you right now. And you don't love me. And I don't want to do anything more than what we've done so far, at least not until I know you better. And frankly, I could do with a lot less of this stuff here. The hugging, the touching, the friendly little kisses you've been giving me."

"But this feels right to me," I told her. "And you're not exactly pulling yourself away in disgust, either. Doesn't this feel at all right to you?"

She kept her palm flat on my chest while running her free hand over my bicep. "Pitt, you're a well-built, very attractive man. Who wouldn't want to feel your strong arms wrapped around them?"

"Apparently *you* don't." I smiled at her. "But like I said, you ain't exactly pushing me away."

"I want to be your friend. You offered me that. And that's all I want." She licked her lips, her eyes drifting to my own, and I knew she wanted more than she was saying. Her body was telling her something different than her heart.

"You sure about that?" I gave her the chance to change what she'd said. "Do you think I can't feel how your body has been heating up ever since I started holding you like this? Do you think I can't feel your heart pounding inside your chest? Do you think I can't see you looking at my lips?"

Her eyes moved up to meet mine. "Like I said, you're very attractive."

"Yeah, just about the most handsome man you've ever seen, right?" I wanted to kiss her so damn bad my mouth ached.

"Yeah." She reached up and took my cowboy hat off her head, then tossed it on the bar. "And I would imagine you're used to getting your way when it comes to women."

I was. But I hadn't wanted to be with anyone in a long time. "Not since my father was diagnosed with cancer over two years ago. I haven't been with anyone—I haven't wanted to."

Her brows furrowed as she looked at me with disbelief in her eyes. "Don't lie to me, Pitt. There's no reason to do that."

"It's true." It felt like the right time to tell her a little more about me. "I had a girl at the time, a long-term girl, but I let her go when I found out my father was going to die. And I haven't gone looking for another woman since. I wasn't looking for one when I showed up here. But now that I've found you, I want more than just friendship. With you, I want more."

"And I want love," she reminded me. "True love."

"Let's see if we can find that, then." I leaned in, holding her tight. Our mouths were only inches apart, her breath hot on my face.

And then she made some weird move and was out of my arms and hauling ass out my door.

CHAPTER 10

Kaylee

After a night of tossing and turning, I got up and got ready for the day before heading out to get some breakfast at The Royal. It was the only restaurant on the island that served eggs just the way I liked them.

As I took a seat at the table I'd spent every morning at so far, the waitress nodded in my direction. She knew what I wanted and went to get it done. I looked out the window, watching the waves roll in.

"Mornin'," came a familiar deep voice.

I turned to find Pitt standing there, his hat in his hands. Then he took a seat at my table without being asked. I looked him over: cowboy boots, blue jeans starched to the hilt, a pearl-snap pale blue shirt with long sleeves. I couldn't help but tease him. "You in town for the rodeo, Pitt?"

His smile was devastating; it was so brilliant. "Funny."

I thought he might be mad at me for running out on him. "So, you're sitting with me. I guess that means you're not too mad at me for last night."

"Mad?" He shook his head. "Not at you. I was kicking myself all night though."

"Figured out you were wrong for rushing me, did ya'?" I smiled to soften the blow.

He nodded and grinned as Petra, our waitress, came up behind him and winked at me. "Good morning." She placed a couple of glasses of water in front of us. "I haven't seen you around here before, cowboy. New in town?"

He smiled at her. "I am," then looked at me. "Have you ordered yet?"

"I get the same thing every morning, so she's already put my order in." I pushed the menu toward him.

"I don't need that." He looked at Petra. "Bring me what she's having. I'm sure I'll like it." He looked at me. "It's not salad, is it?"

I had to laugh. "No, it's not salad. I'm sure you'll like it." I had the day off so thought I might add in something to help calm my nerves, which had started making themselves known with Pitt's arrival. "And how about a mimosa. You want one, Pitt?"

"Orange juice and champagne, right?" he asked.

"That's right." I held up two fingers. "Make it two, please, Petra."

"Coming up." She walked away, and I was surprised when Pitt didn't watch her go. The woman was stunning, after all.

"Did you only bring clothes like that to the island, Pitt?" I wondered how he could stand the heat in an outfit like that.

"I don't own a pair of flip-flops or shorts or any short-sleeved shirts, if that's what you're asking." He ran his hand over the front of his starched shirt. "And I think I look a hundred percent better than anyone here, to be honest with you."

"You do look great." I admired the country look he had going on. "But you've got to be burning up in those clothes. I'm off today. How about we get on a boat and go to Aruba to get some island-appropriate clothing for you?"

The way his lips curled up on only one side made me grin. "Aren't you afraid of being alone with me? That sounds like it might take all day."

I knew I had some teasing coming my way for running away from him like a scared rabbit. "You've proven to be harmless enough. I kind of kicked myself a lot last night, too. I might've overreacted."

"Ya' think?" He chuckled, and the sound came from deep in his chest.

Petra came back with our drinks, and I quickly took a sip of mine. "Yum."

"I'll be right back with your food," she told us then left us alone again.

Putting the long-stemmed glass on the table, I looked out the window. "Sure is pretty outside today. The boat ride over to the next island should be fun, I think."

"So, we're doing it?" Pitt asked me. "You're going to make me buy shorts and silly shoes?"

"I am." I wasn't going to let what happened the night before get in my way of becoming friends with the man. "I think you'll feel more comfortable in something less bulky. Your skin must be craving some sunshine."

"It's craving something alright." The way his sexy grin made my insides quiver just wasn't right.

Petra came back with our plates, and he looked at his with wide eyes. "Um, what's this?"

"Eggs Benedict," Petra answered. "With spinach."

He looked up at me. "There's green stuff on these perfectly good eggs."

"Uh huh." I nodded at Petra. "Thank you. It looks yummy, as usual."

She waited to see if Pitt was going to change his mind. "I can bring you something else if you'd like, sir."

"No. I'll give it a shot. If Kaylee says I'll like it, I'll try it." He looked at me. "And you think I'll like this, huh?"

"You will." I didn't know if he would or not, but I thought that putting the idea into his head might help. "It doesn't normally come with spinach on top, but I like it that way. Spinach isn't like lettuce, it has a distinct flavor to it."

"Yeah," he mumbled. "That's what I'm afraid of. Hopefully the egg will cover up that green flavor I'm sure it'll have." He took a bite and his eyes went wide once more. "Not bad. You were right."

"I know." I didn't know for sure, but was happy he liked it. "What do you usually eat for breakfast? Steak?"

"Just because we raise cattle doesn't mean we eat steak at every meal." He took a drink of water. "But you're right. Lots of times we do have steak and eggs for breakfast."

I laughed a little. "Imagine that."

"Cookie never makes it for lunch, though," he went on. "He packs us sandwiches for that. Usually ham."

"Since I've been on the island, I've stopped eating lunch." I cut into the egg, letting the yolk drip down over the Canadian bacon. "I eat this big, hearty breakfast, and it keeps me going until I get off at four."

"No wonder you're starving by five." He shook his head. "You need to eat more than twice a day. And this ain't much of a hearty breakfast. Back home, Cookie makes a real hearty breakfast. You leave that table needing a nap after his meals."

"Well, you're all probably exhausted from getting up at four in the morning, too." I took a bite and moaned at the flavor.

He stopped what he was doing to gaze at me. "You should stop doing that. It makes it hard for me to concentrate on our conversation."

I felt my cheeks heat with embarrassment. "You're bad."

"I know." He smiled at me, then took another bite.

I began to think that spending the day with the man might've been a bad idea after all. "I'll stop moaning when I eat, and you try to stop enjoying it so much."

The way he looked at me sent chills through me; it was so intense. "I don't think I can stop enjoying the sound of you moaning, honey."

"Would you quit it?" I felt my cheeks heat even more.

"If you really want me to, I will." He looked back down at his plate. "Ugh. I shouldn't have looked at what I was eating. That green just don't sit well with me." He scraped the rest of the spinach off the eggs then put a piece of toast over them. "There, that's better."

"At least you tried it." I shrugged. "That's better than nothing."

"I've got an idea." He grinned at me. "I try something you want me to, then you try something I want you to. Tit for tat."

I blinked at him, already knowing what kinds of things he'd want me to try. "No."

"Don't be so quick to turn me down, baby." He laughed. "And before you get mad again, that's another thing you're going to have to get used to. I'm gonna call you *baby*."

Rolling my eyes, I couldn't believe the man. "You're crazy. Do you know that about yourself?"

"I'm a little crazy." He picked up his glass and looked at me over the rim as he took a drink before putting it back down. "I wasn't talking about anything sexual. I was talking about taking you for a ride later this evening."

"A ride?" I asked, having no clue what kind of ride he meant.

"Galen told me there are horses here." He jerked his thumb over his left shoulder. "He had a few brought in last week. And he wants me to work with them so the guests can ride them. So, wanna' take a ride with me this evening? We can watch the sunset together again."

"Riding with you, on horseback, along the beach, while the sun sets?" I knew I was in over my head. "Sounds like a date, Pitt."

"So does going to Aruba to spend the day together, Kaylee." His chuckle made my heart skip a beat. He had the best laugh ever. I didn't think I would ever get tired of hearing it.

With a sigh, I had to ask, "Can you promise not to try to kiss me again?"

He looked at me with a frown. "Now why would I want to make a stupid promise like that one?"

"Because you want me to come riding with you?" I picked up my mimosa. "Oh, and will I get my own horse, or will I have to ride behind you?"

He pushed his hand through his hair as he looked at me. "You ever ridden a horse before, honey?"

"No." I'd never even been around horses.

With a nod, he went on. "Then you'll ride with me. But not behind me. I don't like that. You'll sit up front."

"Then your arms will be around me." I saw what he was up to. "And you'll be breathing all over me, too."

"Yep." The smile he gave me sent heat right to my core. "My hot breath will be all over that pretty little neck of yours. But I'm willing to suffer through it for your sake."

"Yeah, it sounds like you're really gonna hate it alright." I had to smile. The man was just too damn charming.

And too dangerous.

I shouldn't go anywhere with him.

Sitting there looking at him, I didn't seem to have control over myself as he looked right into my eyes. "So, will you take a ride with me?"

I knew I shouldn't agree. I knew exactly where it would lead— straight to another awkward situation like the night before. But then my mouth opened. "I'll take a ride with you, Pitt."

"Good." He ate the rest of his breakfast without saying a word. I had the feeling he was rushing to get the day over with so he could get me on that horse.

Poor man, he's got a lot of waiting to do.

"I guess I can buy some boots while we're in Aruba. I don't own any." I thought about the pants I owned, none of which would look great with boots. "And I hope I can find some jeans, too."

He stopped eating to look up at me. "You're gonna dress up like a cowgirl?"

"Well, I don't think I should ride a horse wearing shorts and flip-flops." I laughed and got kind of freaked out at the look in his eye.

"Man, you don't know how much I like a girl wearing boots and jeans." He shivered and I laughed. "You're gonna make things hard on me, aren't you?"

"I'm not trying to." I looked, my skin feeling scorched by his gaze.

"Are you sorry you didn't let me kiss you last night?"

I turned to look at him. "I am not sorry about that."

"Damn it." He went back to eating, and I went back to wondering why I was playing with fire.

I'm only gonna get burned.

CHAPTER 11

Pitt

"Y ou can't laugh, Kaylee." I knew how white my legs were from wearing jeans all the time, but she didn't need to point it out.

"I'm sorry, Pitt." She busted into another round of laughter. "But they're so pale, and the rest of you is so tan. It's just too funny."

Stalking back to the dressing room, I took off the shorts and put my jeans back on. "Well, I bet your curly hair looks like a bird's nest when you wake up each morning."

I heard her as she leaned against the door to the dressing room. "You're right. Don't worry about those legs of yours. They'll get tan in no time. At least you can get some sun on your private deck before going out in public wearing shorts."

"I better not catch you taking any pre-tan pictures of me. This is a sight that shouldn't be seen by anyone." I stepped back into my boots then opened the door, holding the shorts out to her. "Help me find five more pairs in this size, and we'll be done shopping."

"You should really try on each pair, you know." Kaylee took the shorts, folding them up and putting them under her arm to hold them for me.

"I am not going to do that." I pointed to the shorts. "That's my size. It fits. Let's find some in different colors, and we'll be done."

We'd already found shirts and some 'damn flip-flops'. I was tired of shopping and ready to get something to eat, then get on the boat back to Paradise.

"I've gotta find some jeans and boots," she reminded me.

"Oh yeah." I scanned her body as I thought how cute she'd look all cowgirled up. "Let me pick them out." Now I'd get to see her trying on everything. "And I'm buying them."

"Nope." She picked up a black pair of shorts, then tucked them under her arm with the khaki ones I'd tried on.

"Yep." I picked up a navy blue pair of shorts in my size and tucked them under my arm.

"I can't let you pay for my clothes, Pitt." She looked at a shirt that had blue flowers over a white background. "This would look great with those shorts you just picked up." She put the hanger over her wrist to add it to her collection.

"Well, I am gonna to pay, so get over it, Kaylee." She headed toward a red pair of shorts, but I shook my head at them. "Nope, not going for red.

"Why not?" She shook them at me. "You'd look good in them."

"I don't want to attract the wrong kind of attention." I took them from her then put them back. "Stick to dark colors, and let the bright ones stay here for some other guy."

"'Kay." She looked around. "We've got khaki, black, navy. Oh, how about white?"

"I guess." Picking out shorts wasn't exactly exciting. But picking out jeans for her would be. "I'm gonna get you every pair of jeans that looks good on you, honey."

"No, you aren't." She shook her head, making her curls bounce around her shoulders. "I'm not supposed to take any money or material objects from any guest at the resort."

"Well, you can lie about who paid for them, can't you?" I asked because I didn't think it was that big a deal.

"No, I won't lie." She smiled at me. "I'm an ethical person, Pitt."

"Well, isn't that special?" I walked toward the counter. "This is going to be more than enough. I'm not going to be wearing shorts much anyway."

"If you say so." She followed me. "I'm just glad you got something you can wear that won't be so hot."

It was nice to hear that she'd been thinking about me and my comfort. "Thanks, babe." I ran my arm around her shoulders then kissed her cheek. "You're a sweetheart."

She held her breath for a second, then let it out. "Yeah, you're welcome."

The way her body tensed let me know I was getting to her. I let her go to get my wallet out to pay for everything. "I'm hungry. Let's get something to eat before we go looking for your jeans and boots."

"I'm hungry, too." Kaylee picked up two of the bags off the counter, and I signed the receipt and picked up the last two. "What're you thinking about eating?"

"Seafood sounds good." I led the way to a little café I'd noticed as we'd walked into town earlier.

"Sounds good to me." She walked next to me, looking up at me. "I'm sorry I laughed at your legs. That was mean." The way she chewed her lower lip had me wondering if she really felt bad about it.

"It's not really anything you need to apologize for, Kaylee." I shrugged. "No harm in a little teasing."

"You sure?" She looked down at the ground. "I've been told I can be mean."

"Sounds like you've been around a lot of whiny little crybabies." I laughed. "I've got thick skin. A little teasing won't hurt my feelings. Not much does."

When she looked back up, there was a smile on her pretty face. "I'm glad to hear that. I mean, I try not to say everything that comes into my mind, but sometimes things slip out. I can be a smartass."

"So can I." I jerked my head toward the café. "This one looks good."

After heading inside, we were taken to a small table for two near the back. The lights were dim, and the decor was on the darker side. "Hello, welcome to Café Dumont," the waiter greeted us in a charming accent. "Our special today is lobster with a white wine reduction sauce. It's served with asparagus tips in garlic butter and potatoes au gratin."

Kaylee looked a little concerned. "How much is that going to cost?"

I held up my hand. "That doesn't matter. We'll have two of those, thank you. And your best bottle of white wine, too. Price isn't an issue."

"I can't let you do that, Pitt," she whispered. "I'll pay half the check. But I don't want to pay a week's salary." She looked at the waiter. "So, what's that going to cost?"

"Never mind." I waved the waiter away. "Don't worry about her. I'll take care of it. You get our order turned in and get that wine coming, please."

He nodded and walked away, and I looked back to find Kaylee glaring at me with her arms crossed over her chest. "Pitt Zycan, I cannot let you pay for my meal. It's against the rules."

"So?" I didn't see why she had to be so obstinate about it. "Who the hell will know about it? I'm not gonna go tellin' anyone; *you're* the only one who could tell that I paid for lunch. So if you don't, we'll be fine." I laughed, noticing that she still looked pissed.

"I thought you said you could be too honest at times." She winked at me. "Seems you don't mind lying at all."

"Look, what I meant was that sometimes I could take the truth a little too far. For instance, when one of my sisters asks me if she looks fat in something, I tell her the truth." I'd gotten into several heated debates with my mother over being too honest with my three younger sisters at times.

Kaylee rolled her eyes. "So, you can be mean, too, I see." Placing her hands on the table, she looked at me. "I like to keep things above board, if you know what I'm saying. I don't like keeping secrets."

I laughed and shook my head. "Kaylee Simpson, you're not exactly an open book who goes around telling everyone your business. I don't think you'll find it hard to keep this to yourself."

"Friends typically pay their own way." She smiled as if she'd won the argument. "You know we're just friends, right?"

Oh, I've had it with the friends *nonsense.*

I decided then and there to let her have things her way for a while and see how long she'd be able to stay just friends. "Sure, we're just friends. I'll let you pay half, and I'll let you buy your own clothes. I wouldn't want to make you think I like you for anything more than a friend, now would I?"

Her face seemed to lose all expression. "Thanks. That'll make things so much easier."

"Great. Whatever I can do to make your life easier, I'll love doing." All I could do was smile at her.

Neither of us talked much after that. We ate, then she nearly had a stroke when her half of the check was a hundred and fifty bucks. After we paid for our meal, we continued with our shopping. She almost had a heart attack when she saw the cheapest pair of cowboy boots was three hundred dollars. And the cheapest jeans were close to a hundred. But she paid for them.

After getting back to the resort, she got off the boat with her bags, and I got off the boat with mine. She looked back at me as she walked ahead. "I'm going to go to my room and get changed. What time do you want me to meet you? And where do you want to meet?"

"I think I'll ride up to your place and pick you up around seven." I headed toward my bungalow, watching her as she walked in front of me.

When she stopped, I did, too. She turned to face me. "That's going to seem like a date, you showing up to pick me up."

"How?" All I could do was sigh. "And so what?"

"So, I don't want anyone to think we're dating." She turned to keep walking. "I'll meet you at the stalls. I'll ask someone where they are, and I'll meet you at seven. Bye. Thanks for the company today, Pitt. I had a nice time."

A nice time?

I had an okay time, but I knew it could've been so much better.

I'd had some pretty great ideas about how our evening would go, but that was before she'd gotten under my skin with the *friend* thing. I thought we'd talked about it, and that she would keep an open mind about being more. But that could never happen if she kept throwing up walls and shutting down anything that even resembled something more than friendship.

But now I had a mission. I'd let Kaylee have her way and see how long she'd be able to keep it up.

The romantic ride I'd planned wouldn't turn out the way I'd hoped. But perhaps it would spur Kaylee on to wanting more than just my friendship. I knew I wanted more, and I was pretty sure that she did, too, deep down. But she wasn't letting me take the reins the way I was used to with most other women.

When she showed up at the barn that evening, she looked puzzled as she looked over the two horses I had saddled and ready to go. "I thought I was going to ride with you, Pitt."

"I thought you might like to ride your own horse. I'll lead it for you until you get the hang of it." I climbed up in the saddle, then grabbed the other horse's reins. "Hop on him and let's get going."

"Um, okay." She looked a little distracted as she reached up to grab the saddle horn. "Like this?"

"Yep, now seat your left foot in the stirrup, pull yourself on up, and throw your right leg over the saddle." I tried not to look at how damn cute she looked in those boots and jeans and her tight-fitting T-shirt. "Settle your feet into the stirrups, and we'll get going."

CHAPTER 12

Kaylee

"And this is important because you're going to squeeze out the juice, getting the most out the fruit." I showed the new girl how I cut the oranges into wedges for the Paradise Blues, my signature cocktail. I was at the bar at the resort's yacht, training a new employee.

"Got it," Lorena said with a nod. "I can see what you're saying."

Looking out toward land, I saw Pitt ambling up the beach with his hands in the pockets of his shorts. His dark hair was damp, hanging in loose curls. He wore the Aviator sunglasses I'd given him a couple of days after our shopping excursion.

It had been a week since our little trip to Aruba, and Pitt had me wondering what had happened to the man who'd been set on being more than just my friend. He and I had seen each other every day, spending time hanging out. We liked catching the sunsets together and seemed to be the only two people on the island who actually wanted to eat dinner at five o'clock. We took that meal together every evening, too.

What we *hadn't* done was move forward in our relationship.

He waved at me and I waved back. He could see that I was busy with the new girl, so I knew he wouldn't come over and talk to me.

"You see that guy?" I asked Lorena. She seemed like a nice girl, so I thought I'd try out the whole 'being open' thing with her. I had gotten used to it with Pitt, but maybe it was time to find some other friends, too.

She glanced up, looking at him for only a second. "Yep." She held out a lemon. "Cut this the same way, right?"

I nodded. "Well, he asked me to dinner the first day he arrived here. I turned him down. But then I felt bad about it and went to apologize and put together a picnic as a peace offering. Anyway, long story short, he tried to kiss me that night, and I ran away. I told him I only wanted to be friends."

She looked at him as he walked by the yacht. "You said no to that guy?" One eyebrow arched. "Are you crazy?"

"Yeah, I think I might be a little crazy." I bit my lower lip as I watched him strolling away. "The next day we hung out together again, and I think I might've been too adamant about us being just friends. He's been good since then, not trying any more moves."

"So, you got what you wanted then." She picked up a cherry. "Leave it whole?"

I nodded, and she tossed it into the glass. "Yes. Anyway, the issue now is that I think I might've spoken too soon; I think I want more with the man. We've been hanging out a lot and being able to get to know him better has opened up my eyes. And my heart, too, I think."

"I bet." She looked at him again. "He looks like quite a catch, doesn't he?"

"Yes, he does." I thought about all the conversations he and I had that week. Nothing deep or intense like those first couple days, but just getting to know each other. Of course, he was much more forthcoming than I, but I did find it easier to talk to him than anyone I'd ever hung out with before.

"So, have you told him that?" she asked me as she went to grab the bottle of coconut rum off the top shelf.

"No." I hadn't had the guts. "I'm afraid he'll tell me that he doesn't like me that way anymore, that I might've missed my shot. I've been myself around him, and I'm kind of a goofball."

"Yeah, I've kind of noticed," she said with a smile. "I saw you at one of the swimming pools the other day. You were jumping off the side and going down the slides and stuff. It looked like you were having a blast."

"Yeah." I felt my cheeks heating with embarrassment. "And I've done other silly stuff with him, too. I pushed him off his deck while he was cooking one night. He got me back though and climbed back out, picked me up and jumped back in with me."

"Sounds romantic alright." She laughed lightly. "Who knows? Maybe that's his way of flirting, or maybe he thinks of you more like a little sister than a love interest."

"You think?" I looked for Pitt once more, but he had nearly disappeared down the beach.

Lorena shrugged. "I've never met the man, so I couldn't say. But it sounds like you don't quite know how you should act with a man you're attracted to. There's nothing wrong with being playful, if that's how you're feeling."

She was right that I had no clue what I was supposed to be doing. "I'm afraid I've been acting kind of childish. I'm already a bit younger than he is, but maybe if I stopped being so goofy, he'd see me as a woman instead of a crazy kid." I knew I'd let him see the real me. And I knew that most people couldn't take a whole lot of the real me.

Lorena looked at me and shook her head. "I don't get you, Kaylee. At work, you seem so reserved. I can't imagine you being so silly with that guy."

I shrugged, not knowing how to explain how comfortable he made me feel. But maybe I'd been feeling too comfortable; maybe I'd blown it by being myself with Pitt. "You know what else I did that I'm now thinking was really dumb?"

She frowned at me. "What did you do?"

"I played a prank on him." I looked down as my face grew even hotter. "I put a balloon under one of the sofa cushions, and when he sat down it popped, and he jumped a foot in the air and screamed like a girl."

Lorena let out a burst of laughter as she shook her head in disbelief. "No, you did not do that to that grown-ass man!"

"I did. And I've done even more stupid stuff, too." I rubbed my temples with my fingertips. "God, I'm such an idiot."

Lorena stopped laughing to give me some helpful advice. "Look, I think you've given this guy a fun time, and it sounds like you have fun with him, too. Would it really be so bad if he did see you as nothing more a friend?"

"What if I kissed him?" I blurted the question. I'd been thinking about going for it for the last few days. Pitt brought out things in me that I'd never experienced before, and at that moment, I couldn't think of a better person to share my first kiss with.

"What if he pulled away?" she cautioned me. "Would you be able to deal with that? Is there a chance that it might end your friendship?"

"I don't know. He's put up with all my stupid pranks and antics, but maybe that would be the last straw." I felt so stupid, saying all of this out loud. I couldn't believe I'd acted like such a fool. "I wonder why he still wants to hang out with me."

"Maybe he's just too nice to tell you to go away," she offered.

I thought she might be right. "Maybe I shouldn't go over to his bungalow anymore. If he comes looking for me, then that's another thing. But I probably shouldn't bother him anymore."

"That could work; it might help you get a better idea of whether or not he still has some romantic feelings about you." She put her hands on her hips as she admired the drink she'd made. "Looks pretty, huh?"

I nodded. "Yeah, it looks great."

When my shift ended I left the bar, leaving Lorena to take the evening shift by herself. And I prayed she wouldn't tell anyone about the things I'd told her.

Walking up the beach to get to my room, I internally berated myself. *Why do you have to be such a goof? Why can't you act like a normal human being? What's wrong with you?*

Maybe I needed to visit the island doctor to talk about getting on some medication that could help me calm down a bit—help me be a bit more normal. I looked up at the sky as I walked, then screamed when I was grabbed by the waist and hauled up into the air. My butt came down on the tops of Pitt's broad shoulders. "Finally, you're off. I've been so bored." He galloped along the shoreline, carrying me on his shoulders as if I weighed nothing.

Holding on tight, I fought the urge to laugh. "Pitt, you should put me own! This is crazy!"

His laughter met my ears. "This is crazy?" He took off running into the water. "You wanna' see something really crazy?"

"Pitt, no!" I shrieked as he kept running until he was chest deep, then he tossed me up high. I tucked my legs in so I could do a cannonball, hoping I'd be able to get him back with a freaking colossal splash. I wasn't going to pass that up.

When I came up out of the water, he was laughing and swimming up to me. "Great cannonball."

"I hadn't planned on swimming." I ran my hand through my hair. "How bad do I look?"

He grinned. "You look a little like a drowned rat." Then he stood up and dunked me.

Yeah, he definitely thinks of me as a little sister.

But it was fun being with Pitt, so I decided to just let it be what it was—friendship.

He hauled me back up out of the water and picked me up in his strong arms, carrying me out of the water. "Hey, I saw on the news that there's gonna be a meteor shower tonight. You should stay late tonight, and we can catch that together."

After we got to shore, he put me back on my feet, and we started walking towards staff housing. "I *am* off tomorrow. I could stay up late if I wanted to."

"And I don't have any cows to tend to, so I can stay up late, too."

He laughed and shook his head. "I'm on vacation. I suppose staying on my strict schedule is kinda' dumb."

I stopped and took his hand. "Pitt, am I rubbing off on you?"

He grinned then tweaked my nose. "Kind of, I guess. You sure are fun, Kaylee."

"You really think so?" I wanted to ask him what else he thought about me. But I didn't because I was afraid of what the answer would be.

"I sure do." He started walking again and let go of my hand. "You're not like most other women I spend time with. You're a real pal."

Pal?

Damn.

"Yeah, I think you're a real pal, too." I ran my arms around myself as a breeze blew over my wet clothes, giving me a chill. "I better get home and get changed before I catch a cold."

We stopped in front of the staff housing building. "See ya' at my place around five then," he said. "I've got some lobsters I'll be grilling. And I picked up a salad from The Royal for you earlier today."

"You did that for me?" I smiled at him. "That was nice of you."

"Yeah, I'm a nice guy." He ran his fingers over my shoulder. "See ya' soon, you little wet rat."

I smacked his hand, then turned to go inside. "Jerk. I'll see you at five."

Walking inside, I stopped after closing the door, then looked out the window next to it, watching him walk away. The way the wet T-shirt clung to his body made my mouth water. I could see the outline of a six-pack, and some prominent pecs, too.

Heading to my room, I mentally kicked myself for putting him in the friend zone. *Why did you have to go and make such a big damn deal about just being friends, you moron?*

Now I had to spend a long evening with the man and not let myself do anything stupid—like try to kiss him.

CHAPTER 13

Pitt

The night we watched the meteor shower, I'd been certain Kaylee was going to kiss me. She'd acted so differently. She didn't joke around or play any pranks. It was like I was hanging out with a different person than the fun, sweet girl I'd gotten to know.

Finally, I'd asked her if she was sick or something, and she only shook her head and told me she should get going.

The following week, she hadn't acted much like herself either. And any time she did start acting like herself, she'd shut it down quickly and get quiet. I didn't like that she seemed to be pulling away from me, so I was on my way to her bar to talk to her about things.

I found a couple of guests sitting at a table and some others who sat along the beach. Kaylee waved at me when I stepped up onto the floor. "Hi, Pitt. How about a nice cold beer?"

"Sure." I took a seat at the bar and pointed to a bowl of peanuts on the counter behind her. "How about some of those, too?"

She placed the bowl and the pint of beer on the bar in front of me. "Here ya' go, cowboy." She looked me over. "Why the cowboy gear, Pitt? It's pretty hot out there today."

I had my reasons for ditching the shorts that afternoon. "I wanted you to see me as the man I was when we first met."

"And why is that?" She looked confused as she picked up a glass to clean it.

"Just did." I took a drink of the cold beer. "You've been acting a little off this last week."

She sighed. "Well, the medication the resort's doctor gave me hasn't evened me out yet. He said it could take a couple months before my body gets used to the medication, but I'm not supposed to stop taking it unless he tells me to."

I knew something wasn't right.

"Why are you taking anything, Kaylee? I thought you were doing fine." She hadn't complained to me at all about how things were going, hadn't mentioned a single time that she thought she needed medication to help her.

"It came to my attention that I'd been acting out a little, so I went to see the doc about my ADHD." She put the glass down then picked up another. "I'm not a little kid. I shouldn't act like one."

"What are you talking about? You like to joke around and have fun; last time I checked, having fun wasn't cause for being medicated." I loved being around the girl and wondered who had made her feel like she was acting like a kid. It sure as hell hadn't been me. "And who gave you this idea that you've been acting inappropriately?"

"It doesn't really matter." She placed the glass on the shelf, then sighed. It was then that I noticed the stool she had back there as she sat down on it. "I hate how I feel. I'm tired and can't think straight. But the doctor said it would even out, and I can't stop taking the pills he prescribed me."

"Look, I'm sure that doctor means well, but Kaylee, I don't see why you need to take anything. Have you really been having trouble managing your ADHD, or is this about something else? You didn't mention anything like that to me, and you've seemed perfectly fine. You're great just the way you are." I hated to see the bubbly young woman feeling this way. "But you're nowhere near the same person now. Can't you see that?"

She nodded slowly. "Yeah. Of course, I can. But I need to follow the doctor's orders, Pitt. I just need to get through this initial reaction to the drugs and then I'll be more like myself. Eventually."

"I wish you would've discussed this with me before you went to see the doctor, Kaylee." I drummed my fingers on the bar as I gave her a stern look. "There was nothing wrong with you in the first place. What did you even tell the doctor to get him to prescribe you something? It just doesn't seem right. You said yourself that you haven't needed medication for years."

She looked at the floor, instead of looking at me. "I told him I was having trouble staying focused at work and that I needed something to help me. Not that it should matter to you; I'm not really your concern, Pitt."

"Kaylee, I'm in here almost every day you work; you're a rock star here." Running my hand over my face, I wondered why she seemed to want me to stop caring. Then it dawned on me. "Do you think that you're not my concern because I'm just your friend?"

She nodded slowly.

I balled up my fists and pounded one on the bar. "Damn it, Kaylee! As your friend, I have a right to be concerned about you and your health."

She looked up at me. "My health is fine. The doctor said all my vital signs are normal."

"Well, you are not acting normal." I couldn't believe that she was actually happy about this—that this is what she truly wanted. "I miss the girl you let me get to know. Do you really think this is what's best for you, honey?"

Tears made her eyes glisten. "Can we talk about this later? After I get off work?"

I nodded, knowing that this wasn't the right place to have this conversation. "I'm gonna hang out here today though. See if I can make you laugh a time or two." I missed hearing her laugh.

Standing up, she turned away from me, and I could tell she was wiping her eyes. "Suit yourself, Pitt. But I haven't found anything too funny lately."

"Since you started taking those damn pills." I took a drink of my beer, then really looked at her. "You've lost some weight, too."

"Yeah, I've only been eating with you." Some guests walked in and sat at table, and she quickly walked over to take their orders.

I hadn't said anything about her eating so little when we'd had our dinners together because I wasn't sure what was going on with her. But to know that all she'd eaten was the little she'd had with me made me feel sick to my stomach.

There were most likely some people who actually needed to be on medication for their ADHD; I didn't think that no one ever needed to be medicated. But Kaylee didn't, of that I was certain. She was more than capable of functioning on her own, and I'm sure she knew it, too—why else would she tell her doctor that her work was suffering?

I had to get her to stop taking those damn pills. They had all but turned her into a zombie. But how could I do that when she wouldn't be honest with me, when she wouldn't let me get closer to her?

The time had come to take our relationship further—and I meant relationship, not friendship. I was well aware what that meant. But I didn't care.

There was no way of knowing if Kaylee would actually stick to her guns about the 'one man' theory she had. All I knew was that I wanted the woman in my life. Every day of my life.

But I had to get her to see that it wasn't right for her to be taking medication. How I was going to do that would be my problem to figure out.

When she came back behind the bar, she reached out and grabbed the edge of the counter. She stopped for a second, closing her eyes. I watched her take a deep breath before opening them and walking again.

"And what was that?" I asked her.

"A little lightheadedness. The doctor said it's a common side effect." She leaned down to pick up a bottle of orange juice, then stood up quickly. Heading to the chair, she winced and closed her eyes again.

"Kaylee, this stuff is making you sick. Are you sure you've told that doctor everything you're experiencing?" I had a very good idea that she hadn't been completely honest with him.

"This is on the list of known side effects, Pitt. He said this would eventually slow down or stop all together."

She looked pale and tired on top of everything else. "Have you been getting much sleep?"

She shook her head very slowly. "No."

"Let me guess—another known side effect." I knew all I needed to know. "I haven't seen one good thing come out of you taking this drug. It's been just the opposite. You're not yourself, you seem sick, and I don't like seeing you this way. I care about you, Kaylee."

"You said we could talk about this later." She got up and started to make some drinks. She seemed agitated, and her body grew tense.

I didn't say it, but I felt like that might've been a side effect, too. "I'll chill." I knew I had to ease up on her.

For the next few hours, I watched her as she slowly moved around, taking orders, messing some of them up, and apologizing profusely for doing so. My heart actually ached for her. And I knew that I cared a hell of a lot for the woman. I cared too much to ignore what was happening to her.

Galen walked into the bar a little later with a smile on his face. "Hey there, Pitt. You havin' yourself a nice time at my resort? I haven't seen much of ya'."

He took a seat next to me as Kaylee placed a bottle of dark ale in front of him. "Good afternoon, Mr. Dunne."

"Good afternoon, Kaylee," he greeted her. "Thanks for the beer, lass."

Kaylee looked at my empty glass. "Would you like another, Pitt?"

I shook my head. "Nah." I wanted to keep a clear head for the talk we'd be having as soon as she got off work. I wasn't about to let her take even one more of those pills.

Galen smiled at me as Kaylee walked away from us. "So, you're sittin' at a bar but not drinkin', huh?" He winked. "Maybe the beer's not why you're here then. Am I right?"

I nodded, then looked at Kaylee. "She's just about the prettiest girl I've ever seen. And the most fun—by a longshot."

"Ah," he said. "I see what's been keeping you entertained for the last couple of weeks."

"Yep." Galen's invitation had made things change in my life. "You know, I've been wondering about all this. I found one of Dad's old hats and put it on. You called and told me to get my tail end to this resort that very day. I take my first excursion to the island and find a little beauty with a sharp tongue working at a bar. And I haven't let her out of my sight much since then."

Galen smiled as he put his hand over his heart. "Have ya' gone and lost your heart to the lass?"

"Well, she hasn't let me get that far yet." I grinned as she looked at me then turned away.

"Playin' hard to get, is she?" he asked.

"No, I think she's not playing at anything. She's just confused about things and pretty hard on herself about certain things. But I see something in her that I can't look away from." I sighed, thinking once again about how the medication was affecting her high soaring spirit. The way she was defending it made me think that maybe that was the real reason behind why she was taking it in the first place.

"And what does she think about you, Pitt?" he asked, then turned the bottle up to take a drink.

"I don't know for sure." And I knew she wasn't likely to tell me what she really thought about me so long as she was on this medication. It was making her as closed off as she'd been that first time I met her. "But I aim to find that out—and soon."

Some woman walked by on the beach, and Galen quickly excused himself to go after her. Kaylee walked back to me after he'd gone. "I hope you didn't tell him about me being on medication, Pitt."

"I didn't." Mostly because I knew she'd hate that. "Kaylee, there's something I've been wanting to ask you for a while now."

She leaned on the bar, placing her chin on her palm. "What's that?"

I looked her right in her golden-brown eyes as I brushed back a few loose strands of her curly brown hair. "Are you about done with this being friends crap?"

She looked at me with serious eyes. "I don't think I'll ever be done being friends with you, Pitt."

Well, shit.

CHAPTER 14

Kaylee

P itt sat quietly at the bar until my replacement came, then he took me by the hand and led me away for what I knew would be a long talk. Or so I thought, anyway. We ended up at the doctor's bungalow with Pitt banging on the door.

I wasn't sure what was happening. The medication had me feeling all out of sorts. I'd thought that getting on something for my ADHD would be the best thing I could do. But it was only making matters worse. I had high hopes that one day the side effects would stop, and I'd be able to get back to normal—only a calmer, less goofy normal.

But Pitt's reaction to learning I was on medication made me wonder if I'd done the right thing.

The doctor answered the door and Pitt immediately told him to tell me to stop taking the medication. He told him that he shouldn't have ever prescribed anything for me, that there was no reason I should be taking anything.

To my surprise, the doctor agreed that I should stop taking that medication, but he wanted me to try another one. Pitt said there was no way in hell that I would start trying something else. And then we left.

I supposed it was due to the effects of the pill that I was simply following along, not saying a thing. It wasn't like me to let other people dictate what my actions should be—but the pills made me feel like someone other than myself.

Pitt took me to my place, demanding I give him the pills, which I did. He tossed them into the toilet and flushed them all down. And then he packed a bag and took me home with him.

"You're going to take the bed, and I'll take the couch." He pulled the blanket down then patted the bed. "You need to get some rest. I'll call Galen and tell him that you've come down with a cold and will be needing this next week off. I figure it'll take about that long to get all that crap out of your system and get you up and running again."

I looked at the bed then at him. "Why are you doing all this?"

"Because I care about you, Kaylee." He walked toward the bedroom door. "Get into your pajamas and get your butt into that bed. When you wake up, I'll have something ready for you to eat. I'm thinking a nice homemade chicken soup with lots of noodles; that should go down easy after a week of hardly eating a thing."

He closed the door, giving me privacy to change. I walked to the bathroom and looked in the mirror. I had dark circles under my eyes, and I'd never been so pale. "You look like a zombie," I whispered to my reflection.

It wasn't like I had the strength to argue with Pitt anyway. So, I got dressed in my pajamas and crawled into his bed. A bed that smelled like him, with a pillow that his head had rested on each night—I had never felt more comfortable and safe.

I fell asleep easily, only waking up when Pitt came into the room carrying a bowl of soup. "Honey, it's been five hours since you went to bed. You need to wake up long enough to eat this soup, then you can go right back to sleep."

Struggling to sit up, I found him putting the bowl down on the side table before helping me rearrange the pillows. "Thank you."

Handing me the bowl once I was settled, he looked at how my

hands shook as I reached out to take it. With a shake of his head, he took a seat next to me. "I'll feed it to you."

"It'll be okay. I can do it," I protested weakly.

"No." He held the spoon to my lips. "Open up."

The truth was that I felt so weak and tired that it was actually easier to let him feed me. "I'm not even hungry."

"You've got to eat."

I knew he would say that, so I opened my mouth and let him feed me until all the soup was gone. "Can I go back to sleep now?" I asked once I was done.

He nodded then got up with the empty bowl. "I'll leave you alone to sleep the rest of the night, but I'm making breakfast for you, and I'll come back in to feed it to you in the morning." He walked out as I snuggled back down, then he came back in with a bottle of water, leaving it on the side table. "Here you go. You might get thirsty during the night. If you need me for anything, just call out to me. I'll be right on the other side of that door, sleeping on the couch."

"'Kay." I closed my eyes, which felt too heavy to keep open. "Thanks, Pitt. No one has ever been this nice to me."

I remembered back when I'd been in high school and had started taking the medication back then. My parents hadn't seemed to be nearly as concerned about how those pills affected me as Pitt was.

His lips pressed against the top of my head then he whispered, "You rest and get back to that girl I miss so damn much it hurts. Night, night. Sweet dreams, baby."

I'm pretty sure I fell asleep before he'd even left the room. When I woke up, it was dark, and I was alone. Looking at the bottle of water, I suddenly found myself dying of thirst and downed the whole bottle.

I got out of bed to get myself another bottle and saw Pitt sleeping on the couch. He was too tall to fit, and his feet hung over the end of it. The blanket had fallen off him as he lay there in his tight boxer briefs. The muscular and lean length of him gleamed in what light there was.

I knew I shouldn't have been looking at his body, so I picked up the blanket and covered him up. Then I kissed the top of his head. "Good night, sweet prince."

I felt a little better the next day, and continued to improve every day. And with each passing day, I knew I was falling in love with the man who hadn't done so much as flirt with me as he took care of me.

At the end of the week, I felt like myself again and wanted to lie on the sandy beach for a while. Pitt obliged me and we sat together as we watched the sun set. "You're like the best guy ever, Pitt Lycan," I told him as we lay there on the soft sand.

"I'm not the best ever," he said with a grin. "But I'll take the compliment."

"No, you are the best ever." I turned my head to look at him. "I don't know another human being who would've done all that for me. My parents didn't even do that for me when I was sixteen and going through the same kind of thing."

His blue eyes drooped a bit. "I'm sorry you had to go through that for so long. A couple of years, right?"

He'd remembered what I'd told him about my past, and that made my heart skip a beat. "You remembered."

"Of course I did." He reached out to brush my hair back. "You had to be on those pills until you were old enough to tell them you didn't want to be on them anymore. And now that I've seen how they make you feel, I completely understand why you didn't want to be on anything. But, baby, why did you think you needed to get back on something that made you feel so awful in the first place?"

There was only the one reason, and I closed my eyes as I finally admitted it to him. "I did it for you."

"What?" He sat up, looking shocked. "Me? What do I have to do with it?"

It was time to fess up. The man had let me take over his home and had nursed me back to health for a solid week. He deserved to know the truth.

"I wanted to be more than just your friend, but you'd started treating me like your little sister. I wanted to make a change, make myself more...normal. I thought if I acted less impulsive, less like a goofy kid, then you would see me in a different light. And I knew I needed medication to do that for me. But it didn't work this time either, and this medicine wasn't the same one I'd been on before. I guess nothing can fix me without making me sick."

"Probably because there's nothing wrong with you." He leaned back, resting his weight on his arm. "You've got a free spirit is all. Having an active imagination, having lots of ideas, and making your ideas come to life are all great things to have. I don't know who or why you were diagnosed with ADHD, but I can't see that it has anything to do with those traits. That's just your personality, and there's not one single thing wrong about that."

"Well, a doctor did diagnose me when I was sixteen. My grades had gone down, and my mind had begun to wander." I laughed as I recalled what my mind would wander to. "There was this boy, Sean Nelson. He sat in front of me in algebra class. He was a senior, and I was just a sophomore then; he was way out of my league. But man, did I have dreams about that guy. I thought about him more than I thought about anything else."

"You do know that's perfectly normal at that age, right?" he asked me with a smile on his face.

"No, I didn't. And when my grades went down, my mother took me to the doctor. She told him how I'd been a very active child and how once I'd reached puberty, I changed. I wasn't as active, and I wasn't as sharp-minded as I'd been. That doctor had asked me all kinds of questions, and I answered him honestly—except for where my mind wandered to. I only told him that I had a hard time concentrating and my mind would move elsewhere often."

"You should've been honest with him, Kaylee. I'm sure he would've known you were just a horny teenage girl." He laughed, and I reached out to smack him on the shoulder.

"Was not!" I sat up as I shook my head. "Look, I did read up on ADHD in teen girls, and I thought that's what I had, too. And the truth was that once I started taking the medicine, I didn't think about that guy anymore."

"That's because those types of drugs have the side effect of taking away your sex drive. That's the only reason you stopped thinking about him." His eyes lit up. "And I bet that's exactly why you've held onto your virginity for so long. You weren't exactly holding out for Mr. Right. You just weren't interested in having sex."

"Hold on." I'd been off those pills for years. "Pitt, I only took them for a couple of years. I got off them when I turned eighteen. I do want to hold out for the right man—and that has more to do with my heart than my sex drive. And I do believe that I can wait a little longer for that to happen."

"What makes you think that?" he asked with a knowing grin.

I closed my lips tightly. *Should I tell him how I feel?*

The *what if's* started popping up in my head. Like, what if he laughed at me? What if he didn't feel the way I did? What if I made a complete fool of myself?

"Have you ever been in love, Pitt?" I decided to ask him that first.

"Once, I thought I was in love." He looked up at the sky which had gone dark and was filled with stars. "But when I let her go so easily, I knew it wasn't the kind of love that one needs to make things last forever."

So he had felt some type of love before. I knew he could feel it again—hopefully with me. So, I went for it and just prayed he'd found some love for me.

"Pitt, I know I can hold out for the one man who's right for me, because I'm ready now. I've fallen in love with you."

CHAPTER 15

Pitt

She's in love with me!

Rolling over, I cupped her face in my hands. "I'm in love with you, too." I felt like I'd been waiting to say it for so long that I couldn't wait a second longer.

Her chest rose as she took a sharp breath. "God, I'm glad to hear you say that."

I moved in closer as she lay on the sand. "Does this mean I can finally have that kiss I've been craving?"

But her hands moved up to grip my wrists. "Pitt, you know what that means for me, right?"

"That I'm the one man for you." I nodded as I gazed into her eyes. Eyes that I could imagine myself gazing into forever. "And you're the one woman for me."

"You won't leave me when your vacation is over?" she asked with wide eyes.

"We'll figure things out. I don't want you to worry about that, baby. Now shut the hell up and let me kiss those sweet lips of yours."

"'Kay," she whispered, then closed her eyes.

Never had I felt so much adrenaline running through me as when I looked at Kaylee, waiting for her very first kiss. I had to make it one to remember.

Softly, I touched my lips to hers, letting her feel the sparks flying through her body the same way they were flying through mine. Already a fire had begun deep inside of me, a fire that had been smoldering for what seemed like forever.

I pressed my lips a little harder to hers then parted her lips with my tongue. Her tongue met mine, and they began gently rolling around together, and she moaned. Her arms curled around me, holding me tight—like she never wanted to let me go.

As I ran my hands up and down her arms, I knew I'd found her. *The one.*

I'd never thought about anything like that before. I'd always known some people believed in that stuff—in soulmates—that there was one person for everyone. I'd never put much thought into it before, but as we kissed and touched each other, I knew it was true. I pulled my mouth away from hers to kiss her neck. "I'm never letting you go, baby. Not ever."

"I never want you to let me go." She moaned as I kissed a line up her neck, then nibbled her earlobe.

"This is going to be one for the books, baby. A love worth being written about." I pulled back to look into her eyes. "You believe me, don't you?"

"You're my sweet prince." She ran her hands over my cheeks. "I'll believe anything you tell me."

I'd never felt so deliriously happy before. I took her mouth again, and this time I let the kiss go wherever it wanted. Our hands were everywhere, touching, stroking, fondling. And my growing cock was making itself uncomfortably known.

She took my hand, placing it under her shirt and then moving under her bra. I groaned with the pleasure of getting to feel her plump tit and taut nipple for the first time. "Oh, baby. You feel so good"

Rolling over with her, I moved her on top of me, her soft core grinding against my swollen cock. Her body was hot with desire and so was mine. I looked first to one side, then the other to make sure we were alone on the dark beach.

Kaylee noticed what I'd done, and she smiled as she sat up on top of me. "I think out here would be the most amazing experience I could ever dream of." She moved her body back and forth, stroking me to arouse me more.

But I had to be sure she really was ready for this. I took her by her arms, putting a halt to her movements. "Kaylee, are you one hundred percent sure that you want to do this?"

Pulling her lower lip between her teeth, she nodded. "I am sure that I want you to make love to me on this beach. One hundred percent positive, Pitt."

I growled as I turned her over, pinning her to the ground. Then I quickly set my erection free before undoing her shorts and pushing them down, along with her panties. I could feel the heat coming off her virgin cunt already.

"Shit!" I'd just recalled a certain crucial fact.

Her eyes went wide. "What is it?"

"I don't have any condoms." I smacked myself in the forehead. "Damn it!"

She only smiled at me. "I'm on the pill."

"Holy shit. That's great news, baby. And I know I'm clean." I kissed her again as I helped her shimmy all the way out of her shorts, freeing her legs to wrap around me.

I slid my erection along her wetness, and my whole body shivered, knowing she was so ready for me. Then I sank my hard cock into her as she gripped my biceps.

I kept the kiss going as I moved inside of her, feeling her legs tighten around my waist, moving gently so she could get used to my size. The way her nails dug into my arms let me know she was in a fair amount of pain, but I was certain that it would ebb quickly.

Her walls were so tight they actually hurt me a little. We'd both be sore in the morning, that was for sure. But we'd both be pretty damn happy in the morning, too, when we woke up together in my bed.

When she started moving her hips in rhythm with me, I knew the pain had passed, and that we were headed to uncharted territory for my girl. I wasn't about to give up until she was out of her mind, until she was having her first orgasm. The thought alone almost made the whole experience end way before either of us were ready.

Moving my mouth off hers, I kissed my way up her neck. "You okay, baby?"

She moaned as she ran her hands up my arms then over my back as her foot ran up and down the back of my leg. "I am now. That first part was on the rough side, but now—well, now it's like nothing I could've ever imagined."

"Glad to hear that." I bit her neck playfully. "I've gotta admit that I've never felt anything like this, either."

"I'm all tingly inside." She moved her hands back to my biceps. "And your muscles are crazy sexy, babe."

"I aim to please." I kissed her again, knowing I was taking her higher and higher until she was shaking and moving her mouth away from mine.

She screamed with her release. "Pitt! Shit! Oh, God!" Then she moaned, and I couldn't hold it back any longer.

"Yes!" I shot my load into her as I made the most horrific sounds I'd ever made. "Fuck!" My hips were still thrusting gently, beyond my control with the intensity of my release. "What did you do to me?"

"What did you do to me?" she asked back as she moaned some more.

Once our bodies had stopped all the tingling and pulsing, I rolled off her, lying on my back, looking at the stars. "You're going to have to be careful, baby."

Kaylee got up, grabbing her panties and putting them on. "Careful? About what?"

I leaned up on one elbow, watching her as she put her shorts on, too. "Careful with my heart. It's yours now. I've never given it away before. You've gotta be careful with it. Promise me that you will."

She laughed and held out her hand to help me get up. "I promise you that I'll be very, very careful with your heart, cowboy."

After tucking myself back into my shorts, I took her hand and let her help me up. Then I scooped her up and carried her to the bungalow. "You're staying with me from now on. You know that, right?"

She put her arms around my neck then laid her head on my chest. "I wouldn't want it any other way. We've got some things to figure out, don't we?"

"What's to figure out?" I asked as I smiled down at her. "You'll be coming home with me."

"Well, not right away, I'm not." She looked up at me with a serious face. "I don't want to rush into anything."

"We'll see. We've got a while before we have to make any decisions." I kissed her, then said, "For now, you're staying with me."

"That's a given." She reached out to open the door, then in we went. Kaylee turned to me with a sly smile. "And it's also a given that we're going to be doing a lot more of what we just did, right?"

"Oh, hell yeah." I kicked the door closed then carried her to the bathroom. "Like right now. We're going to take a shower and get all cleaned up."

"And then I bet you aim to get us all dirty again," she said with a sexy knowing grin.

"Now, how'd you know that?" I kissed her again before putting her on her feet.

She pulled her T-shirt off over her head, standing there in her bra and looking sexy as hell. "I think I've got ESP." She pushed her shorts down, leaving her panties on.

I pulled my shirt off, and she gasped then stepped forward to run her hands all over my muscles. "You like?"

"Very much." She bit her lip. "Pitt, we're going to have a tough time getting out of that bed."

"I know." I dropped my shorts and underwear on the floor, then twirled my finger for her to turn around. "Let me get that bra undone for you."

She turned away from me, lifting her curls up so I could get to the hooks that held up her big tits. "I never thought this would be so easy.

I never thought I would feel so free with anyone. I'd pictured this kind of thing going very differently."

I kissed her shoulder as I slipped the strap down her arm. "I feel free with you, too. This is easy, isn't it?"

"So easy." She turned to face me, and I grabbed both sides of her panties, ripping them off her. "Pitt!"

"What?" I looked, seeing that her face had gone an adorable shade of pink. I pulled her close to me, so our bodies were flush with one another's. "I love you, Kaylee Simpson. I never want you to doubt that."

She ran her fingertips over my cheek as she looked into my eyes. "I love you, too, Pitt Zycan." I could feel her heart racing, our bodies deliciously skin to skin for the first time. "This is crazy how I feel. Is it supposed to feel this way?"

"What way?" I asked, but I knew what she would say.

"Like I'm flying and on fire at the same time. But I also feel safe. It's a mixture of things." She looked at me with bewildered eyes. "How's that even possible?"

"It's not a thing one tries to understand." I ran my hands through her hair. "Don't try to analyze it. Just let yourself feel it."

"I feel like my heart's about to pound out of my chest." She closed her eyes. "I feel like I might just pass out from excitement."

"I doubt you'll pass out, baby." I laughed, letting her go so I could turn the shower on. "But if you do, I'll give you mouth to mouth."

Reaching out, I took her by the hand, pulling her into the warm shower with me. She looked up at me with an expression I'd never seen on her. Pure love is the only way I could describe it. "I hope this never ends. I really do. I can't imagine how horrible it would feel if this ever ended."

"Well, you don't have to worry about that ever happening." I pulled her into my arms, then kissed her softly. But what she'd said stuck with me. I'd never suffered from heartbreak before.

And I hope I never do.

CHAPTER 16

Kaylee

The sound of seagulls calling out woke me up. Dim sunlight came through the blinds, and I turned to look at Pitt sleeping next to me. My breath caught in my throat, and I felt my heart skip a beat.

The rays of sunlight highlighted his handsome face in a way that made my heart melt. I never could've imagined what this would feel like.

True love.

It felt like this feeling would never end. I knew, without a shadow of a doubt, that I could get past any differences we might have in the future. The love I held for the man would be so much greater than any aggravation or disagreement we could ever face. The fact that he loved me just the way I was made things that much sweeter.

I wanted to do something nice for him that morning, our first morning together. Although what I really wanted to do was snuggle back into his arms and spend the entire day doing what we'd done all night, I knew I should get up and get us some sustenance.

As I moved my legs to get out of bed, I felt tremendous pain and stiffness in my lower region. Stifling a loud moan so as not to wake Pitt, I clenched my jaw and closed my eyes as I got out of bed.

Limping to the bathroom, I prayed I wouldn't walk this way the whole day. Looking in the medicine cabinet, I was thankful to find some ibuprofen that would help the soreness, and hopefully the stiffness, too.

After cleaning myself up and taking the pills, I went to the kitchen to make breakfast. I wasn't much of a cook, but I could make toast and scrambled eggs. So I got to work doing what I could.

Pitt had said something about women learning to cook to bag a husband, and I thought I might start making it a point to learn how to cook more things. Not that I was trying to get Pitt to marry me just yet, but I knew that would come—in time. I didn't want to be the kind of wife who expected her husband to cater to her in every way.

As I set to work, cracking eggs and buttering toast, I felt domesticated for the first time in my life. Like a real Holly Homemaker kind of girl. That felt good, too—surprisingly. Pitt made me feel better than I knew possible—even while doing something as mundane as making a small breakfast.

I stood there, stirring the eggs as they cooked, when suddenly I felt hands move around my hips, drawing me back into a hard body. Warm breath flowed across my neck as soft lips kissed my nape. "Morning, gorgeous."

My body melted into his. "Good morning to you, my sweet prince."

"You're cooking." He chuckled. "And it doesn't look half bad, either."

One of his hands moved past me as he pushed the pan off the burner, then turned it off. I found him turning me around to face him. "So, you're not hungry?" I asked.

"I'm hungrier for you than anything else." He picked me up and sat me down on the countertop facing him. "I had fun last night. Did you?" His hands moved up and down my arms as he gazed into my eyes.

At that moment, I was really thankful that I'd gotten up before him and had fixed my unruly curls, washed my face, brushed my teeth, and slipped into one of his T-shirts and a pair of panties. He'd only managed to put on a pair of boxers and get his teeth brushed. His dark curls were disheveled, but it only served to make him even sexier.

I ran my hands through his thick hair as I gazed back into his blue eyes. "Fun? I guess you could call it that." My lips ached to feel his on them again, and I leaned forward.

The way his hand moved to cup the back of my neck as the other moved along the middle of my back gave me chills. Our lips met, and I instantly went wet for him. When he moved in closer, pressing his pulsating cock against my sex, I gasped at the way my body responded so quickly, my every nerve pulsing.

I had no idea if sex with anyone else would've felt as good as it did with Pitt, but I had to say that sex with that man was out of this world. And I never wanted to try it with anyone else. I felt like I was made for him—only him.

His mouth left mine, leaving my lips tingling, then he kissed his way over my shoulder as he pushed the T-shirt up to uncover one of my breasts. I moaned as his mouth closed over it, licking it, then sucking gently. Moving my hands over his muscular back, I couldn't believe what we were doing. And I couldn't believe we hadn't been doing it since we'd first met.

Damn, I've been missing out.

"Pitt, I'm so sorry that I just wanted to be friends in the beginning. This is so much better."

He moved one hand to play with my other breast as he moaned, "Mhmm."

"Who would ever think that having your tits sucked would feel so good?" I placed my palms on the countertop behind me and leaned back, stretching my body to give him as much access to my tits as he wanted.

Pulling his mouth off me, he stood up, then picked me up in his arms. "Allow me to show you something else that feels good, baby."

I wrapped my arms around his neck as he carried me to the bed, setting me on the very end then pushing me to lie back. I felt a little nervous as he stood there, looking down at my body. "What're you gonna do, Pitt?"

"You just close your pretty brown eyes and relax." He went to his knees then pushed my legs apart.

I couldn't close my eyes; I had to see what he was going to do next. "Are you going to..." I hesitated to say the words.

He finished them for me. "Kiss you in the most intimate way?"

Gulping, I nodded. "Is that what you're going to do?" I shivered as I thought about him being down there with his face all over my twat. I wasn't completely sure about this. "Maybe I should take a bath first and shave all the hair off? I'm not ready for this. I haven't prepared at all."

Pitt shook his head then grabbed each side of my panties, ripping them off. At this rate I wasn't going to have any left. "Nope. You ain't goin' nowhere. You're perfect just the way you are. I don't go for all that hairless crap on my account. I like a woman who isn't afraid to be natural, the way God made her."

"Yeah, but—" I had to stop talking, my breath leaving me as his lips pressed against my clit, making electricity zap me there. "God!"

He rubbed the insides of my thighs as he ran his tongue through my slit, and I couldn't help but close my eyes and moan with desire. He groaned, and it vibrated through me in a way that sent me even further into ecstasy.

"Oh, what have I been missing?" I couldn't believe I'd willingly passed this up for so many years.

I'd thought having sex the usual way—missionary— had been the best there could ever be. I hadn't counted on Pitt doing much more than that. And I would've been completely satisfied with what we'd done all night. But now that I knew his intimate kiss could rock my world even more—well, I had all kinds of kinky ideas running through my brain.

"You're going to make me into such a bad girl, Pitt." I fisted the sheets in both hands as he stuck his tongue into me, thrusting it in the same way he'd worked me with his hard cock.

He growled again, and it sent even more vibrations deep inside me, and I screamed. I arched my back and the floodgates opened, spilling my juices right into his mouth. He licked, sucked, and slurped it all up, leaving me breathless with shock.

Wiping his mouth with the back of his hand, he looked at me as I lay panting on the bed. "You taste amazing, baby. Would you care to see how I taste?"

My eyes flew open as I looked at him with surprise. "You want me to suck your dick?"

"I would like that very much as long as you're game." He smiled as he dropped his underwear to the floor.

"Pitt, I don't have the slightest clue how to do that." I shook my head. "What if I accidentally bite you?"

With a deep chuckle, he said, "I trust you not to do that to me."

I didn't trust myself. But he didn't seem to have any doubts as he lay down on the bed on his back. His hard-on stood straight up, and I gulped. "It's so big. Do you think it'll choke me?"

That earned another chuckle. "If it does, you can stop. You won't die, you know."

"What if I throw up?" I had all kinds of ideas going through my head about what might happen. "You know when your semen shoots into my mouth? What if it makes me sick?"

"I guess we'll just have to see what happens as we go." He sat up, pulling me up to lie beside him. "Here," he stroked my back then pulled my hair back in one of his hands, holding it out of my way. "I wanna watch you do it."

"Damn, Pitt." I opened and closed my mouth a few times to stretch it. "If I do it wrong, just tell me."

"There's no wrong way to do it, baby. Having you touch me in any way will always feel amazing. Just move your lips over your teeth to sheath them. Move your head up and down; I'll help you with the speed. And relax and enjoy getting to know me better." He smiled sexily at me. "My bets are that you'll like doing this."

"I hope so." I did want Pitt to be pleased with me. But more than that, I wanted to share my body with him, and have him share his with me, in every way imaginable.

I leaned over as he stroked my back and placed a tender kiss on the tip of his erection. "Hold it with both hands, baby. Slide your hands up and down it, covering where your mouth has left."

"Okay." I did as he said and before I knew it, I was giving my first blow job. Once I settled into a rhythm, I really started to enjoy myself. In fact, I loved it.

He growled and groaned and called me sweet names as I sucked him off. "God, Kaylee, you're remarkable. I can't believe you've never done this before. You're amazing, baby. Keep going, keep going, I'm almost there. Just a little..."

He made the sexiest sound I'd ever heard—and I'd heard him make some great ones—then liquid heat shot down my throat so fast I didn't have time to think about what I was doing. I drank it all down, then pulled my mouth off him, wiping it with the back of my hand.

His eyes were closed as he rested his head on the pillow behind him. I couldn't recall a time I'd ever felt so satisfied. "So, that was okay?"

The way he shook his head slowly made my jaw drop. "That wasn't okay at all. That was the most exhilarating thing I've ever had done to me."

Oh, okay then, a compliment. That's better.

CHAPTER 17

Pitt

The months flew by with Kaylee sleeping in my bed every night. We'd grown closer than I knew possible. We were the kind of couple who could finish each other's sentences, the kind who could have fun doing just about anything together.

We went on a deep sea fishing trip, had gone snorkeling, and even swam with dolphins. And each trip seemed like the best time of my life. And it was all because she was there with me.

We sat out on the deck only a couple days before I was supposed to leave. The moon had risen, the stars twinkled, and I pulled Kaylee closer to me, hugging her as we lay on one of the lounge chairs together. "I don't want to leave you, Kaylee."

She laughed then kissed my cheek. "Then don't. Stay here with me in Paradise."

"Okay." I knew I couldn't really just forget about my family in Colorado. "There is the ranch to think about, though."

The sigh that left her body made me think she wasn't crazy about the ranch taking me away from the island. "I still don't fully understand you, Pitt. You've got more money that you could spend in a life-time, yet you're still set on working that ranch."

"Yep." I kissed the top of her head. "It's in my blood. I've told you that before. And it's in the blood of my family, too. My grandfather would be overwhelmed without me."

"I can see why you wouldn't want to let him down. I love my one remaining grandparent. Grampa Richard is the only one I've got left. He's retired though, so he doesn't need anyone to help him do anything."

She looked up at me with twinkling eyes. "I'm lucky to have him still. He used to take me to the dollar store on Saturdays when I was a kid. He'd let me pick out ten dollars worth of whatever I wanted. After that, we'd go eat at the Dairy Queen near his house, and I'd spend the night with him, giving my parents their Saturday night date. Grampa and I would stay up late watching television; he loved those old westerns."

"When's the last time you saw him?" I asked her, squeezing her gently, loving the way her body melded with mine.

"Right before I left to come to the island. I went to see him just before I took a cab to the airport. He told me I had to come back to visit when I got time off." She looked at me again. "But now I think I'd like to spend my vacations with you at your ranch."

That was sweet of her—but what I wanted was a lot more than that. "How about you come live with me and go see your family as often as you'd like to? We've got a private jet; you could see them every week if you wanted to."

"Live with you?" She raised her head then shook it. "It's too soon to do all that, Pitt."

"You live with me now." I didn't see the problem. "So, what makes it any different than what we're doing now?"

"I've got my own job, my own money. I still have my freedom." She shook her head again. "I'm not ready to give that up."

"Who's asking you to?" I wasn't about to treat her any differently than I did here on the island. "I don't make you sit by my side every minute of the day. You've got your freedom. And you always will have that freedom. Hell, baby, I just told you that you could get on the jet and go see your family whenever you want. I won't be able to go with you every time you go. I think that's giving you plenty of freedom. I'm not into trapping you, anyway."

She still wasn't thrilled with the idea. "It's only been a couple of months, Pitt. That's moving way too fast. I think we can see how things go. You can hop on that jet of yours and come to see me as often as you want to. And I can spend my vacations with you. My family will understand."

"Have you told them about me, Kaylee?" I had no idea if she had or not. We'd never discussed that before.

"I haven't had a chance to." She laughed a little. "I'm not hiding it from them or anything. I'll tell them soon enough. I've just been so busy with going to work and spending the rest of my time with you. Mom didn't expect tons of phone calls anyway. I've never been big into talking on the phone."

I hadn't told my family anything about her either. "I see what you're saying. I haven't taken the time to call home either. You've taken my attention right from the start, you little vixen."

"Vixen?" She laughed as I tickled her ribs. "Not really."

"You are, too." I tickled her more, and she wiggled and laughed. "You're a sexy little vixen who played with me until I captured you and made you mine."

I stopped tickling her and watched her catch her breath. "You did make me all yours." She ran her hand over my cheek. "What will life be like without you around?"

"Unbearable." I kissed the tip of her nose. "Come on, baby. Living with me will be great, I promise you it will."

"Even if I wanted to, it's a bit more complicated than just saying yes. There's the fact that you've got to leave in two days, and I would need to give at least two weeks' notice to my manager." She shook her head. "I can't just leave them short-handed like that."

"That's nice of you—thoughtful even." I thought she needed to be reminded of something though. "But most of the guests will be leaving the island when I do. So, you don't really need to give that much notice. There are plenty of bartenders left to take over your shifts."

Concern filled her eyes as they darted back and forth. "Pitt, there's still college. I want to go and get a degree, and I'll need money to pay for that. And before you even offer, I don't want you to pay for it. I want to do it myself."

"Noble girl, ain't ya'?" I had to admire her spirit. But I kind of hated that it got in the way of what I wanted.

"I don't know about that. I just know that I want to work for my money. I want to pay my way through this life, not have it paid for me." She sighed as she snuggled into my chest. "I don't know what the right thing to do is. I'll admit that. The thought of spending even one night without you is giving me anxiety."

Me, too.

I had to figure out something. The girl wanted to pay her own way, and I liked that about her. No one could ever accuse her of being a gold digger. My family would respect her for that.

But I wanted her with me at the ranch. "I'm sure you could get a job in Gunnison."

She looked at me with one arched brow. "Not one that would pay as much as this place does. It's a lot, Pitt. I mean, way more than I could ever make as a bartender in the States."

"I could pay for some of your college, couldn't I?" I had to try something. "I mean, as your boyfriend, don't you think it's okay for me to help you out? I would let you help me out if it made you feel better. You could do my laundry and put it away if you wanted, and I would pay you for doing that."

"A good partner would do that for you sometimes anyway, wouldn't she?" Kaylee wasn't going to go for anything simple like that, I could see that now. "Might as well tell me you'll pay me for making our bed and keeping our bedroom clean."

I had to laugh. "Yeah, it sounds pretty weak, doesn't it?" But I really didn't want to leave her there. "I just want you with me so badly. Don't you want to be with me?"

"I do." She took a deep breath then let it out. "Pitt, I'm only twenty-two. I'm young. And being young, I don't know if I want to jump into something as permanent as moving all the way to Colorado with you and throwing away the kind of money I can make here. It might be a terrible mistake. It's just too early to know if we're meant to be together forever."

I'd had no idea she had doubts about us. It left me a little shocked —and a little pissed off. "Kaylee Simpson, are you saying that you think I might not be the man for you? Because I've got to let you know that that hurts like hell to hear you say such a thing to me. You told me you were holding out for the one man who would be in your life forever. I assumed that when I kissed you that night on the beach that meant that I was that man."

"And I think you are. I really do." She sat up and looked at me with eyes that said she'd told the truth. "Please don't take this the wrong way, babe. I love you so much. I'd kill and die for you. All I'm saying is that I'm young. What if things change between us? What then?"

I had no idea what to say to that. I'd thought we would be together forever from the moment I kissed her. "I don't think that will happen, baby. I've never felt this way about anyone. This is rare, what we have, I can promise you that. I know I'm not in my twenties, but I've been there. I understand what you're saying. And I get it. You don't want to depend on my money. You don't want to let that hold you to me because you wouldn't have any way to support yourself if things didn't work out the way we think they will right now."

She nodded and smiled at me. "Yes, that's it exactly. I want to pay my own way through school. I want to have my own career. I want to always feel that I'm taking care of myself. I don't want anyone to take care of me financially. I'm glad you see what I'm saying."

A thought crept into my head, but I had to say it in just the right way, or I knew she'd reject it. "Well, what if you could have a job in Gunnison that would not only pay you enough to get that degree, but that you could also turn into a business afterward that you could run using that degree?"

She looked a little confused. "Do you know of a place there that would do that for me?"

"Well, there's not one right now, but I could make that happen for you." I had to find the right words, and I was having trouble. "I could buy a bar. You could run it for me, manage it. I'd pay you a good salary—equal to whatever they're paying you here. And once you graduate, you could buy the bar from me, and then it would be all yours."

She just looked at me as her brain took that all in. But then she shook her head. "No, thank you. That would still be me letting you help me. I want to do this all on my own, Pitt. Please understand."

"So that's your final answer? You won't be coming home with me?"

How could I leave this place without her?

CHAPTER 18

Kaylee

The next morning I woke up with Pitt's arm draped over me, and one of his legs, too. I was trapped in bed with the man who seemed to be having a hard time letting me go—even for just a little while.

Easing his arm off me, I tried to do the same with his leg and failed. He snorted as he woke up. "What're you doing, baby?"

"I've gotta pee. Let me up." I wasn't thrilled about telling him why I needed to get out of bed so badly, but he'd gotten so clingy the last few days.

"Oh, okay." He moved his leg off me, then turned over to go back to sleep.

I went to the bathroom and looked in the mirror. "What are you going to do about this situation, young lady?"

There wasn't a single doubt in my mind that I would miss Pitt like crazy. I dreaded the next day—the day he'd be leaving. But somewhere inside of me, I knew he could stay with me if he really wanted to. There were other people who could work at that ranch. And more could be hired to take his place.

Turning on the shower, I found myself mad that I had to go to work that day while I had the next day—the day Pitt had to leave—off. Once he left I'd be all alone, and that bothered me more than I ever thought it would.

I would have to go back to my room, and I'd probably spend the whole day in there—crying most likely. And all because he wouldn't stay with me.

Sure, he'd suggested I go home with him, and he'd come up with that crazy idea about buying me a bar, but I couldn't see that in any other light than another way of letting him take care of me.

I'd left home pretty soon after I graduated from high school and turned eighteen. I've always wanted to be independent, and I'd never had any intentions of living off anyone but myself for the rest of my life.

My Grampa Richard had talked quite a bit about how it was important for a woman to maintain her independence. That way, she would never feel stuck in any relationship. He'd seen too many women stuck in abusive relationships in his time; he'd been a marriage counselor for fifty years. So, I had to take the man's words seriously. He'd seen it with his own eyes, after all.

A part of me hoped that Pitt would go back to his ranch, realize he didn't have to be there, and then come back to me. Maybe he could buy a bungalow from Galen, and we could live happily ever after right here on the island.

But then I thought about how selfish that idea was and felt bad about my hopes. There seemed to be no compromise that the other would be okay with. And that had me worried.

I already wasn't in the best state of mind. Anxiety had been building since the beginning of the week as I tried to figure out what we were going to do. I didn't want to lose Pitt, and I know he didn't want to lose me, either. But we weren't breaking up or anything like that. It would just be some temporary time apart.

Maybe we needed that to make sure we were meant to be together. If he left me and went back to his home and realized he hardly thought of me at all, then he wasn't as in love with me as he thought. And I thought the same thing about myself. How was I to know if I truly loved him unless I spent some time away from him? I was certain that would help me know for sure.

The bathroom door opened, and Pitt went to the toilet and started peeing. "Are we really at this place, Pitt?" I turned my back so I didn't have to see him doing something like that.

"We are." He laughed then flushed the toilet. "You can be so squeamish sometimes, baby." He got into the shower with me. "Let me wash your hair. I love doing that."

"You just called me squeamish for not wanting to watch you pee —as if that's somehow weird." I smacked his hand as he reached for the shampoo.

"I didn't ask you to watch me. I just think it's fine if you got used to me doing that while you're in the bathroom. And I want you to feel free to come in and do your business when I'm in the bathroom, too. There's nothing wrong with that—especially if we're going to spend the rest of our lives together. I'm sure we'll see each other in much worse scenarios as time goes by." He picked up the shampoo bottle and poured some into his palm. "Now turn around and let me wash your hair for you."

With a sigh, I turned around and thought about what he'd said. "Do you really think we'll be spending the rest of our lives together, Pitt?"

"Well, we have some obstacles we have to get over first." He kissed my shoulder. "Like you not wanting to come home with me."

I sighed, trying to think of how else I could explain to him why it was so important to me to stay on the island. "Have you stopped to think that what you want is a little selfish? I'd be changing my whole life around, while you wouldn't have to change a thing."

"I don't think of it that way at all." He massaged the soap into my hair, and it felt so wonderful.

I'm going to miss this so much.

"Well, I should've known you would say that." Of course, the man didn't think he had a selfish bone in his magnificent body.

Pushing my head back, he rinsed the shampoo out of my hair as I closed my eyes. When I felt his lips touch mine, my body reacted as it usually did when he kissed me: my legs went weak, and I felt as if I was melting.

His arms ran around me, pulling me close to him as he held me. When our lips parted, he looked at me with those dazzling blue eyes of his. "Would it make you feel more comfortable about coming home with me and letting me pay for things if you and I were married?"

What?

"Pitt, no." I pushed against his chest. "Let me go. It's hard to think when we're all skin to skin like this."

"I don't know if I want you to think." He let me go anyway. "And why are you so quick to say no to marrying me?"

"It's too soon." I picked up the conditioner only to have him take it from me.

He poured some into his hand then handed the bottle back to me. "I know I want to be with you from now on. Why not make it official? And that way you'll have half the money I have. It'll be all yours, too. I can even set up an account that'll be just for you."

"I don't want that." He had no real idea what I wanted, no matter how many times I tried to tell him. "That's very nice of you, but that's not what I want."

He massaged the coconut-scented conditioner into my hair as he sighed. "I know. It's just that tomorrow I've got to leave, and it's got me all mixed up. I'm getting desperate here. Can we, at the very least, come up with a plan for when we'll get to see each other again?"

"Well, I've got to work for a week after all the guests leave, and then I get two weeks of vacation." I thought being apart for a week would be plenty of time to see how being apart would affect our feelings for each other. "How about I come to see you for those two weeks?"

"Okay." He turned me around to face him, then kissed me tenderly.

It felt good to have this decided. I didn't like all the tension that had come between us with not knowing when we'd see each other again.

But going to see him meant that I couldn't go see my family. That was the only drawback to the decision.

He pulled his mouth off mine and smiled as he pushed my head back to rinse my hair. I knew I had to say something about seeing my family, but wasn't sure how to word it. "Do you suppose we could take your jet and go see my family for a couple of days before I have to come back here to work?"

His smile went clear across his face. "You bet that would be okay. More than okay. I want to meet your family, Kaylee."

"Good." I felt relieved. "And I want you to meet them. I can't wait to meet your family, too." I meant that, though I was a little afraid that they would think I wasn't high enough on the totem pole for him. "Do you think they'll be okay with me, even though I'm not rich like you guys are?"

"Hell, baby, none of my family thinks like that. They'll love you. I can promise you that." He pulled me back into his arms and swayed with me. "Just so you know, I might not let this marriage thing go as easily as you think."

"Why would you want to hurry up and get married, Pitt?" I couldn't understand him. I thought most men didn't want to rush into marriage. I'd heard that women had to drag their husbands down the aisle, not the other way around.

"I've got my reasons, honey." He smacked my ass, and the sound reverberated off the shower walls.

"Pitt!" I yelped.

All he did was grin at me. "I was thinking that after you get off work, we could spend the rest of our time together playing slap and tickle until I have to get ready to leave. What do you think about that?"

I thought my body would spontaneously combust. Heat filled me as I thought about all the things we could do. "You're going to make it hard on me at work today, you know that? All I'm going to do is think about what you've got planned for me."

"Good." He smacked my butt again. "Cause I've got a few more things to show you before I have to be away from you for a week. Things that'll have you hating our time apart, that'll have you rethinking your decision to not move to the ranch with me."

"You're not going to make this easy, are you?" I didn't have to ask him that. I knew he wouldn't be taking it easy on me. It wasn't in his nature.

"Honey, let me tell you this much: I've been holding back the really great stuff for this night." His hands moved in slow circles all over my butt. "You'll be begging me to let you come with me when I'm done with you."

"I hope you won't be upset when that doesn't happen." I had to laugh.

He just shook his head. "I'm serious. You're going to wonder how the hell you'll ever live a day without me, darlin', I can promise you that. You have no idea what I can do for you."

I had a very good idea what he could do for me. He'd done miracles for me so far.

What more can there be?

He put his hands on my waist then lifted me up, pinning my back against the tiled wall. "I'll give you a little preview now. Right now, I'm going to hold you up, and you're going to put your legs over my shoulders. Then I'm going to eat your sweet pussy until your juices are dripping down my face."

I looked down at him with disbelief. "Damn, Pitt."

He nodded. "And after that, I'm going to put you on your hands and knees on the bed and take you from behind, spanking you as I fuck you relentlessly."

I couldn't believe the way he was talking to me. And I couldn't believe how my body was shaking with anticipation. "Oh God."

"I will make you *see* God, baby." He put me back on my feet, and I had to hold onto him, my legs too weak to stand on their own.

I don't know how I'm going to get through this workday.

CHAPTER 19

Pitt

I'd never hated seeing the sunrise until that morning. The day had come that I had to leave the island and get back to the ranch. And Kaylee hadn't changed her mind about a thing.

I knew that a week wasn't the lengthiest amount of time to be apart, but it wasn't sitting well with me at all. I'd woken up with a knot in my throat. *A damn knot!*

I'd never cried over any girl in my life, but there I was, waking up with a knot in my throat and tears burning the backs of my eyes. It seemed crazy. Especially since she would be coming to see me in a matter of seven days.

Deep down inside, something whispered that there was a chance she wouldn't come. Something said to me that what I wanted could never be. And that was killing me.

I stood on the deck, watching the last island sunrise I'd see for at least a few months. I wasn't sure how long I could hold out. I also wasn't sure how fair it would be to my family if I kept leaving the ranch to come to Paradise every few months to see Kaylee.

The ranch is where I belonged. If Kaylee couldn't ever come to terms with that, then I had no idea what kind of a future we had together. And so far, she was set on keeping her job and staying right where she was—except during her time off.

I knew we'd never last if things stayed that way. But getting her to understand that had proved impossible so far.

Small hands moved around my sides and I felt her body sidle up behind mine. "You should've woken me up, Pitt. I wanted to watch the sunrise with you."

"You looked so peaceful, sleeping like that." I turned to take her into my arms and kissed her softly.

Kaylee stood on tiptoe, then I picked her up, and she wrapped her legs around me. She was wearing one of my T-shirts, which I'd told her she could keep so she could sleep in it after I left—so she could think of me each and every night. I walked inside with her, kissing her all the while.

Taking a seat on the sofa, I put her on my lap. Only then did I notice her lack of panties. She tugged the waistband of my underwear down, then ran her hands up and down my cock until it was hard as a rock.

Our mouths parted as she looked into my eyes, lifting her body up then sliding down on my erection. "One last time before you have to go."

I didn't like to think about leaving. The knot formed in my throat again. I pressed my forehead against hers as she clenched her thighs to make her insides contract around my cock. "Baby, you've got no idea how hard this is."

"I do." She pulled her head back, then held my face in her hands. "Just let me look at you. I want to remember every last detail about this handsome face of yours. This week is going to go by like molasses, I know it is."

Not wanting to seem like a love-sick fool, I tried not to beg her again to come with me. And I couldn't believe how hard it was not to cry. But some manly part of me held those tears back as I lifted her to stroke my cock. "I love you, Kaylee Simpson. Please don't forget that. I love you more than I've ever thought humanly possible. I'm going to count every second until I see you again."

She smiled. "Seems you'll be spending our time apart wisely." Her hands moved off my face, moving to run through my hair. "You're probably going to get this cut before I see you again. I want to revel in the curly thickness of it before you cut it off."

"I could leave it for you." I thought better of it. "Or better yet, you could just come with me, that way you can make sure I don't cut it."

Her eyes sparkled as she shook her head. "This is going to be good for us. I have a gut feeling."

"I think you're wrong. I don't want to leave you here. Everything in me is telling me to toss you over my shoulder and take you with me." I pulled her hands to my lips, kissing each knuckle.

"Caveman." One tear fell down her cheek, making my heart stop.

I couldn't stand to see her cry. And that one tear brought the protective man in me back to life. "Hey, it's only a week, baby." I wiped the tear away. "Then I'll be in Aruba to pick you up. The jet will take us back to the ranch and later on the week after that, we'll go to Austin to see your family for a few days. It'll be fun. We'll take them out to fancy dinners and stuff like that."

She choked back her tears. "Yeah?"

I nodded. "Yeah."

She kissed my cheek. "You know I can't let you spoil them. You're not supposed to spend money on me, remember?"

"I won't be a guest on the island anymore," I reminded her. "I can spend all the money I want on you once I leave this place. And I'll buy you whatever I want to."

"Pitt, you're crazy." She laughed as I moved her hips faster, up and down.

"Over you, I am." She would see, I wasn't going to let her control everything once I left the island. "We've got to exchange cell numbers before I leave. Don't you let me forget about that."

Panting, she nodded. "Will do, boss. Now shush." She put her hands on top of my shoulders, hanging on as her body began to clench around me. "Pitt!"

Her sweet juices poured around my cock, making things nice and slippery. "Oh, yeah, baby. Give it to me."

I kept going until my balls got tight and my cock jerked as I came hard inside of her. Once she'd caught her breath a little, I heard her giggle faintly. "Good thing I'm on birth control," she whispered, "or I'd be knocked up for sure."

Looking at her, I knew I wouldn't mind knocking her up one bit. "Maybe we can think about planning a baby sometime in the not-too-distant future. A little mini-me running around might be nice."

"Another you?" She laughed then kissed me before adding, "I think that sounds nice, too. We'll have to see where things go and what we come up with before we go making baby plans."

I cupped her cheeks, trying to memorize every bit of that pretty face. "We'll make this work. I swear to you that we will. I'll do whatever it takes to keep you in my life. And I will make you my wife. You can count on that, Kaylee Simpson. One day, you'll take my last name, and we'll have us a houseful of kids with that last name, too."

"You know what I've never had, Pitt?" she asked me with a smile.

"Nope." I lifted her up high. "Tell me, and I'll make sure you get it."

"I've never had a dog. Mom's allergic to them." She reached down, running her fingers through my hair.

Bringing her back down to sit on my lap, I pushed my hand through her unruly curls. "I'm sure I can get you a puppy. That'll be our practice kid. If we take good care of it, then I'll let you have your real baby."

She smacked me on the shoulder, the way I knew she would. "You don't get to *let* me have anything, Pitt Zycan."

Her feistiness never got old. "Oh, yeah?" I got up, tossing her over my shoulder. "We'll see about that. For now, though, it's a shower for us. We've gotta' clean up, and I've gotta pack up. And then comes the hard part. You better not make me cry when you say goodbye to me at the dock." I smacked her ass, making her yelp.

"Pitt!" I put her on the floor after turning on the shower then pulled the T-shirt off her as she bit her lower lip.

"You know what?" I asked her. "I want you to keep all my summer clothes here. I won't need them back home. And that way I'll have some clothes here when I visit you. What do you say about that?"

She shook her head. "I don't have enough room for that. My closet is small, remember. And there are only three dresser drawers, too. You'll have to pack them up and take them with you. But I do want to keep one T-shirt. I've gotta' wear it to go to sleep, or I'll probably go crazy."

I knew I was going to go crazy without her in my bed. "And how am I supposed to sleep? And don't offer me a pair of your panties to wear. That's just weird."

The water ran over us as we bathed, and she seemed to be deep in thought about what she should give to me. Then her eyes lit up and she pulled a bracelet made of tiny shells off her wrist. "Hold out your hand." I did so, and she put the bracelet on my wrist. "There, you can look at this and think about me. I hope it gives you sweet dreams."

I hoped it would, too. I was pretty damn sure that all I would dream about was her. "Thank you."

Way before I was ready, the call came that Galen's yacht was leaving. I had to meet him at the dock and leave Kaylee behind. We held hands as we walked to the dock, and I realized I was still wearing shorts and a T-shirt. "My family will get a kick out of me showing up wearing this."

Kaylee rested her head on my shoulder. "I bet they will. I can't wait to meet them. Tell them that for me."

"I will." I kissed the top of her head. "Be good, okay?"

"I will." She pulled her cell phone out of the pocket of her shorts. "I almost forgot."

"Shit. Me, too." I pulled mine out and we exchanged phones, adding our information into each other's contact list.

When she handed mine back to me, I saw she'd put her name as *Kaylee, the girl you deflowered at the beach.* Smiling, I nodded my head toward her phone, which she now held. "Okay, Kaylee, the girl I deflowered at the beach, check out what I put myself under."

She looked at her phone and laughed. "Okay, *Cowboy Lover.*"

It felt good to laugh with her when all I wanted to do was cry. I put the phone into my pocket and looked at the yacht that had already docked. "I bet Galen is already on the boat." The steward came to get my luggage. I knew the time for goodbye had come.

One sweet kiss, then I let her go. "I love you."

She nodded and bit her lower lip, trying to keep the tears away. "I love you, too." Her head dropped. "This is a lot harder than I thought it would be, and I already thought it would be hard as hell." She laughed a little. "Turns out it's hard as fuck."

"I know." I didn't want to put too much pressure on her, but the words came out anyway. "I hope this will be the last goodbye we have to say to one another. Please take this week to think about coming to live with me."

She looked up at me with glistening eyes. "I promise to think about it, Pitt. Now, you give me a call when you make it home safely. I don't care what time it is, you call. I won't be able to sleep until I know you're safely on the ground and back home."

"Ah, you really do love me." I smiled at her, then turned to walk away. "I'll call you. Don't worry. As soon as I walk into my front door, I'll give you a call. Love you, baby."

"See you in a week. Love you, too, my sweet prince." When I looked back, I saw she'd turned away and was running as fast as she could. I knew she was crying and didn't want me to see.

That damn knot came back into my throat again, but I knew her tears were a good sign for our future.

CHAPTER 20

Kaylee

My heart hurt so bad I thought I might die. I couldn't catch my breath I was crying so hard, and it had been nearly an hour since Pitt had left. "Why can't I quit crying?"

I put a pillow over my face as I lay on my bed and kicked my feet with frustration. I knew I would be seeing the man again in a week. How could his absence be affecting me so badly?

Getting up, I went to the bathroom to wash my face. When I looked in the mirror, I gasped. "Damn! What the hell?" My eyes were swollen, red, and soaked with tears. "Kaylee Simpson, you've got to get a hold of yourself. You're going to see him again. He'll be calling you when he gets home." I had no idea what time that would be, but I knew he would call. And then we could talk on the phone every day.

That helped me a little. I stopped crying, anyway. Sure, my heart still felt like I might be having a heart attack, but at least I'd quit crying. I still looked like hell, though.

I thanked God that I didn't have to work that day. Anyone who saw me looking like that would think I was a little insane, if not thoroughly unwell. And if anyone asked me why I'd been crying, and I told them that I'd turned down Pitt's marriage proposal and the opportunity to live with him, they would know I was nuts.

And maybe I was crazy. I felt kind of crazy for letting him go all alone. I wondered for a split second if he'd come back for me before the week was up. But then I knew he wouldn't. He had the ranch to see to.

Maybe I'd been stupid not to realize that he needed to be a part of that ranch. And who was I to get between him and his family?

I could find a job in Gunnison, and I could save up for college. I could do it all right there with him. But I was being stubborn, holding out hope that he would decided he wanted to stay on the island with me. He could never be completely happy living on the island.

How could I not have realized that until just now?

Sure, my job paid more than any other bartender job I'd ever heard about. Did that make it worth living without my true love?

Hell no, it doesn't.

I'd been dumb—and yes, even immature. But I was over it. I would go to him in a week, and I would stay with him. I needed to let Mrs. Chambers know, but that would have to wait just a bit longer. I looked at my reflection again. "Because you look like complete shit."

Heading back to my bedroom, my heart felt a little less heavy as I plopped down on the bed. Then my cell rang, and my heart sped up, hoping it was Pitt. But when I pulled the phone out of my pocket, I saw it wasn't him after all.

"Mom?" I answered the call. "I've been meaning to call you. I've got some great news."

"Sweetie, I'm so sorry, but I've got some terrible news to tell you," she said, and I could hear the tears in her voice. "Your Grampa Richard is dead."

The world began spinning as I felt a wave of shock move through me, filling my entire body. "No."

"I'm afraid so." She burst into sobs, and I heard my father as he took the phone from her.

"Dad?" I cried.

"I've already called the airlines and booked you a flight out of Aruba this evening. You'll get to Miami around three in the morning. Then there's a commuter jet from Miami to Austin. You're scheduled to arrive in Austin around eight-thirty tomorrow morning. We've got a lot going on here, as you can imagine. I've taken care of renting you a car, too. You've still got your key to our house, right?"

"Yes," I whimpered.

"Okay then, you should have just enough time to go home and get a shower before you come to the funeral home. You remember the one your grandmother was in, right?" he asked me.

"Yes." I couldn't believe it. My grandfather was gone. I would never get to see him again.

"Okay. Well, you've got a lot to do, sweetie. You'd better get busy. I love you, and we'll see you in the morning."

"Bye, Dad. I love you, too." I swiped the screen to end the call then tried hard not to fall apart as I hurried to get my things packed. I had so much to do and not enough time to do any of it.

Packing everything into my suitcase, I knew I wouldn't be coming back. The funeral and all that entailed would take up the week. From Austin, I would go to Pitt in Colorado. I might even ask him if he would come to Austin to be with me during the hard time that lay ahead of me. I knew it might be selfish, but I wanted him with me. I needed him to be with me.

Grampa and I had been closer than I'd been with any of my other grandparents.

Now I'll never even get to talk to him again.

The tears started flowing all over again. This time for my Grampa. I remembered the way we'd talk when watching those old westerns, and he'd tell me how he rode horses all the time when he was a little boy.

I'd thought about how cool it would be to take Grampa to Pitt's ranch to show him all the animals there. And now that would never happen. He would never get to meet the man I loved. He would never get to meet the kids we'd eventually have.

And all I could think about was that if Pitt was with me, I could bury my face in his broad chest and let him help me through all of this. But I'd let him leave me behind.

It occurred to me that he was on a private jet, and if I'd have gone with him, we could've just turned the plane in the direction of Austin and been there way earlier than the next morning. But I had stayed put.

I felt foolish and sick to my stomach. Twice I had to run to the bathroom to throw up, that's how upset I was by it all.

Knowing I had to leave something telling my boss where I'd gone and what I was doing, I sat at the small desk and got out a pad of paper and a pen. I wrote that I had to leave and that I wouldn't be coming back. I made sure to thank them for the job and tell them that I'd had a wonderful summer. But that's all I could get myself to write. I couldn't think straight.

After packing, I put on some sunglasses then set out to see if I could find a boat that would take me to Aruba. As I reached the dock, I saw the Jamison's stepping onto their yacht. "Hey, you guys think you can give me a lift to Aruba?"

Mrs. Jamison nodded and waved. "Sure, come on. We're just about to leave."

I hurried to get onto the boat, then placed my luggage on the deck. "Thank you so much."

Mr. Jamison looked at me with concern. "You alright?"

I shook my head. "No, sir." I couldn't talk very well as I kept wanting to cry anytime I opened my mouth. "I'm sorry, it's hard to talk about."

Mrs. Jamison seemed to understand. "That's fine, dear. You don't have to say a thing." She took my hand, leading me to the cabin. "Here you go. Take a seat in here, and we'll be docking in Aruba in about an hour. Do you need a ride anywhere once we get there?"

"To the airport." I chocked back a sob.

"We'll get you there." She patted me on the back. "We have our jet there. Do you need us to take you anywhere?"

"No. I've got a ticket waiting for me. Thank you." I closed my eyes, wishing I was alone so I could cry some more.

Seeming to sense that I wanted space, Mrs. Jamison left me. "My husband and I are going to be in our bedroom on the lower deck. It looks like you could use some time to yourself."

I nodded, then put my face in my hands, trying not to cry too loudly. Nothing was going the way I'd thought it would.

When we docked in Aruba, the Jamisons let me ride with them to the airport, then I got on a plane just as the sun left the sky. When they told us to put our cells on airplane mode, I knew I would miss Pitt's call, and that made my heart ache even more.

Sitting in my seat next to the window, I looked out as we left the ground. Only then did it dawn on me that I could've sent Pitt a text about meeting me in Austin at the airport.

I needed him so damn bad it almost didn't make sense. All I could think about was that if he held me in his arms, this wouldn't hurt so damn badly. If he were with me, things would be okay. But he wasn't, and I'd been so upset that I hadn't thought about anything else.

Somehow, I fell asleep on the ride to Miami. The stewardess woke me up after all the other passengers had gotten off the plane. "Excuse me, Miss, we've arrived in Miami."

My eyes flew open. "Shit!" I knew I'd have to rush if I were going to catch my connecting flight.

I had to get to the luggage terminal and grab my bags, then get to the next gate, which turned out to be at the other end of the airport. I was out of breath when I reached the gate, and I was the last passenger to board.

Gulping as I took my seat, I prayed that my luggage had made it on board, too. I patted my purse. "At least I've got this. My ID, my house keys, and my cell phone."

The stewardess came to me as I pulled the phone out. "No, no, Miss." She pointed to the light that had just lit up. "No cell phones until we land."

I nodded as I put the phone away in my purse.

CHAPTER 21

Pitt

Walking into my bedroom back home on the ranch, I'd never felt more alone. I missed Kaylee already and knew it would only get worse when I had to spend the night alone.

I'd made it home safely and was eager to call her to let her know. Pulling the cell out of my pocket, I got ready to hear her sweet voice and hoped it would be enough to get me through the night.

When the call went straight to voicemail, I couldn't believe it. "What the hell?"

I tried calling again just to be sure. Again it went to voicemail without even ringing. I knew that meant she'd turned her cell off, but what I didn't know was why she'd done it.

It was nine at night, my time. That made it eleven at night where she was. Sure, that was a little late, but she'd told me to call her no matter the time. *So, why did she turn her phone off?*

A sick feeling started crowding into my stomach. I went to take a shower and get ready for bed. My mind sped with a bunch of disturbing scenarios for why I couldn't reach Kaylee. I wondered when I'd developed such an active imagination—maybe it was just one more way that Kaylee had rubbed off on me. I thought about everything from a shark attack to the possibility that she'd changed her mind about us—that she'd just been telling me what I wanted to hear before I left her.

As I dried off, I shook my head as I looked at my reflection in the mirror. "No, she loves you. Don't go thinking she didn't mean it. She's the most honest girl you've ever met."

Making my way back to the bed, I looked at my cell laying on the nightstand. Picking it up, I prayed I would see a missed call from her. But there wasn't one.

Calling her one more time, I found that nothing had changed. I felt as if an arrow had gone straight through my heart as I heard her voicemail one more time. With nothing else to do, I got into my bed, looking at the empty space beside me where I'd had high hopes Kaylee would be occupying soon.

I turned my head, staring at my phone for a moment before picking it up and tapping in a text telling her that I'd made it home just fine and that I looked forward to hearing from her in the morning when she woke up. I ended the message with the words *I love you and always will.*

A part of me thought she might've just cried herself to sleep and forgot to charge her phone. That's the only way I was able to fall asleep—the idea that she was laying in her bed in her room, phone in her hand, making little snoring sounds and completely unaware that it had run out of batteries.

That has to be it.

Four o'clock came too quickly, and it was a struggle to get up after having slept in for months. I yawned, stretched, and looked at my cell that lay on the nightstand. The first thing I did was check to see if I'd missed Kaylee's call, then I tried calling her again.

Straight to voicemail.

"Fuck!" It was early, and I knew she might not be awake yet. But my heart still ached, and I was still worried about what could've possibly happened in the hours since I'd left her.

After getting dressed, I headed out to get on a four-wheeler and start back at my normal workday. Mom sat at the kitchen table, waiting for me with a pot of coffee brewing. "Morning, stranger." She got up and came to hug me.

"Mornin', Mom." I wrapped my arms around her, lifting her off the ground. "I missed you."

"I've missed you too, Pitt." She ran her hand over my cheek once I'd put her feet back on the floor. "Look how tan you've gotten. And I see a change in your eyes, too. You've let it all go, haven't you, son?"

With a nod, I went to pour myself a mug of coffee. "I finally had my chance to grieve Dad properly." I chuckled. "He—or better yet—his voice came to me when I first arrived on the island. He told me that I shouldn't waste my time there mournin' him—that I had to move on. It turned out he was right, and that was exactly what I needed to hear to find some peace. And I met someone there, Mom."

"A girl?" She clapped her hands. "A special girl?"

"The most special girl in the whole world, Mom." After filling my mug, I placed the cap on it so I could take it with me, and then turned to see the reaction on my mom's face. "She's the one, Mom."

Mom's jaw dropped and she put her hands over her mouth. "The one?"

"Yep." I took a sip of the hot coffee. "She's going to be coming here next week. And if I can get her to stay, I'm keeping her with me forever. I'm gonna marry that girl."

"Does she know this? Have you already proposed? Did she say yes?" She took a seat at the table and looked like she was about to get down to some serious wedding planning. "We can have the wedding here. The ballroom would be perfect for that. I thought your father was crazy when he said he wanted to add that room, but now it all makes sense. What better place to start a marriage? Oh, Pitt." She got up and ran to hug me again. "I'm so happy for you!"

"I did ask her to marry me, but she said it's too soon. So I wouldn't go making too many plans just yet." I let her go, knowing that I had to get going. "But she'll be here next week, and we'll see if I can get her to marry me as soon as possible. I can't wait to change her last name."

"You look happier than I've seen you in a very long time, Pitt." Mom walked back to take a seat at the table again. "I can't wait to meet her."

"She can't wait to meet you, too. She told me to tell you that." With a quick nod, I went out the door to the garage and hopped on a four-wheeler to get to the barn.

It looked like I was the last one to show up, as most of the horses were gone. I looked at Ol' Red, a ten-year-old gelding who stared back at me as I walked into the barn. "Hey, Ol' Red, what ya' been doin', boy?"

He whinnied at me, and I knew he was happy to see me. After saddling him up, I hopped on, then took off to see what the morning would hold for us.

Checking my cell about every half hour, I decided to try to call Kaylee again when six o'clock rolled around. That meant eight in the morning, her time. "Alrighty, Ol' Red, let's see if my girl has woken up yet."

Voicemail again.

Now I was getting even more worried. Kaylee usually got up around six most mornings. She was just about as dedicated to those sunrises as I was. Eight was the latest she'd ever slept the whole time we'd been together. So why was she not up yet? Why hadn't she seen that her phone had died?

I gave it two more hours then tried to call her again. And still, I got nothing. So, I went one step further and called the manager of the resort. Galen had given me the resort number while we were on his yacht heading to Aruba. He said that if I had trouble getting through to Kaylee's cell phone for any reason, I could call the manager and she'd get her for me.

"Camilla Chambers, Paradise Resort. How can I help you?" she answered.

"Camilla, this is Pitt Zycan."

"Oh, yes. You just left us yesterday. I hope your trip home went well," she sounded like she was smiling.

"It went fine." I tried not to let the worry leak into my voice.

"I've been trying to call Kaylee Simpson. She told me to call her once I got home safely, but she hasn't answered. I think her phone might be out of battery, and she hasn't realized it yet. Do you think you could send someone to tell her I'm trying to get in touch with her?"

"Oh, I'm sorry. I can't help you, Mr. Zycan," her answer confused me even further.

"And why is that?" I couldn't believe she would deny my request. "You know we were staying together the last couple of months, right? We're together. We didn't break up or anything."

"Yes, I knew you two were together." She sighed. "Look, all I know is that she wasn't in her room when one of the other girls went looking for her this morning."

My heart stopped, and I leaned my elbow on the saddle horn so I could rest my head on the palm of my hand. I felt weak all of a sudden "She wasn't there?"

"No, sir," she replied. "She left a note, though."

"A note?" I couldn't believe what I was hearing. "Is she not in her room? Or is she not on the island?"

"She's not on the island. She left, and she quit her job, too." Camilla sighed again. "I don't know what happened or I would tell you."

"Can you tell me what the note said?" I asked, looking for any clue as to why she'd leave without telling me what she'd planned to do.

Camilla sighed again. "It just said that she was sorry, she had to leave and wouldn't be coming back. No one saw her go, so we're all at a loss here. And I'm worried, too. The only number I have for her is her cell, and I've only been getting her voicemail, too."

"Don't you have a number you can call in case of an emergency or something?" I knew most employers did, and I didn't imagine Paradise would be any different.

"Yes," Camilla told me, giving me some hope. "It's her grandfather's number. She said her parents travel a lot, and they wouldn't be great candidates for receiving emergency calls. I've called her grandfather's number a few times, but it just rings and rings. It's a landline, I'm pretty sure, and there's no answering machine."

"Is there an address?" I asked, praying that there was.

"Well, she did give me her home address." She'd raised my hopes again. "But this was the apartment she'd been living in before she came to work here. She'd told me that she'd let that go, since she would be living here. I don't have anything else on file for her. If we were anywhere else, I would think about reporting her missing. But we're on this remote island, and it's apparent that she left of her own accord."

"How would she have left the island though, Camilla? Someone must've taken her to the mainland." I clenched the cell as anxiety grew inside of me. "Something's not right. I can feel it."

"What time did you leave?" she asked. "And she did see you off, didn't she?"

"She was with me at the dock, yes." I tried to recall the exact time I'd left. "It was ten after one in the afternoon. So she had to have gotten a ride sometime after that. Do you know who else left after that time? And do you know how to get in contact with them? I've got to talk to whoever took her away from there. I've gotta know where she is." I was going nuts not knowing where she was, not knowing what had happened.

I heard a sound as if Camilla was tapping a pencil on top of her desk. "I'll have to ask around. We don't make everyone check out the way a normal resort does."

"Maybe you should change that," I offered my advice. "Ask around, and then please get back to me. I'm in Colorado, in the mountains, so sometimes I lose signal. Text me the information and the number I can call as soon as you know, please."

"I'll get on it." She hesitated. "Mr. Zycan, I'm just as concerned as you are. But I think that she may have wanted to go back home. This might've been too much for her."

"I hope you're right. I look forward to hearing from you, Camilla." As I ended the call, I knew something was really wrong.

What could have made her leave the island?

CHAPTER 22

Kaylee

As soon as I got off the plane in Austin, I had to find the nearest restroom so I could once again be sick. My nerves were a wreck, and it had made my stomach feel like a million of butterflies were flying around, and a good number of vampire bats as well, taking a nip at me now and then.

I barely glanced in the mirror, knowing my reflection was horrifying. The puffiness around my eyes had hardly lessened. The whites of my eyes were bloodshot, and my overall color was pale.

Digging through the carry-on bag I'd packed, I got out a baseball cap to cover my awful curly mess of hair. Then I found my sunglasses and put them on to hide my eyes. I had to get to the car rental place inside the airport, then get on my way to Mom and Dad's to try my best at cleaning myself up and making myself somewhat presentable.

My stomach growled, letting me know it needed food. "No time, tummy."

Making my way to the other side of the airport, I wondered why in the hell everything seemed to be going wrong for me. Every damn airport I'd been in had me going from one side to the other. To say I felt unlucky just didn't cut it.

A headache started to creep up on me, probably because I hadn't eaten in so long. I rubbed my temples, trying to ease the ache as I kept on toward the car rental place. It suddenly occurred to me that I hadn't picked up my luggage yet. "Shit!"

Turning back, I had to backtrack all the way back to the luggage carousel where I found that my two suitcases were the only ones left. Feeling like a real idiot for forgetting something so important, I then realized that I was kind of in a daze.

Slowing down, I grabbed the handles of my luggage, pulling them along behind me on their wheels.

Thank God for suitcases with wheels.

I felt so weak that I didn't know what I would've done if I had packed a different suitcase. Carrying two heavy bags all the way to the other side of the airport would've been nearly impossible for me at that time.

When I arrived at the counter of the car rental place, I found no one around. Looking every which way I could, I found no one. I hit the bell on the counter anyway and was shocked when a guy came out of nowhere. "Morning. What can I do for you?"

I looked at the wall he seemed to have come out of. "There's a door there?"

He nodded. "I know. Weird, huh?" He tapped on the computer and then looked at me. "So, what can I help you with, Miss?"

"Um, my dad set me up with a rental here." My stomach gave a loud growl and my cheeks heated with embarrassment. "Sorry."

The guy just smiled. "No problem. His name is?"

I stood there, trying to think of my father's name but drawing a blank. "Oh, Lord, I've forgotten Dad's name."

"Long flight?" the guy asked me with a knowing expression.

"Several long flights." That wasn't the only reason I was spacing out. "Um, last name is Simpson. Does that help?"

He clicked away then smiled. "It does if your father's name is Gary Simpson."

"Yeah." I nodded. "Gary—yeah. That's Dad."

"Okay, he's set you up in a compact car." His fingers flew over the keyboard. "I'll need to see your driver's license, please."

I got it out of my purse and waited for him to write down all the information he needed. "What kind of car is it?"

"It's the most economical car we carry." He tapped away some more, then handed my driver's license back to me. "Thanks. The car is electric. It's a smart car."

"One of those tiny cars?" I asked him.

"Yeah. It seats two and there's enough room in the back for your bags." He printed out a paper then pushed it to me. "Just sign this, and you can be on your way."

I signed and then he took me out to my car. I managed to put my things in myself before getting in the driver's seat to start heading toward my parent's house. As I pulled away from the airport, I realized it was the first time I'd been alone in many hours.

My mind started wandering to thoughts of my grandfather. He'd taken me and some of my cousins on a fishing trip when we were all in our early teens, and it was a memory I'd always cherished. Our grandmother was alive back then, but she didn't want to go on the trip.

My cousin Lacy and I were the only girls. Our other three cousins were boys and older than us. Grampa had made sure they didn't tease and torture us too much. Lacy had caught the biggest fish that day, and I had caught the smallest. We both got prizes for our wins. She got to pick where we ate dinner that evening, and I got to choose where we got ice cream afterward. My cousin Jeff told our Grampa that every time he took us somewhere, we all had a blast. We all declared that Grampa was the most fun Grampa ever. The smile didn't leave the old man's face that whole night.

The idea of going to the funeral home and reminiscing with my relatives seemed daunting. So many tears would be shed. I wasn't sure how I would be able to take so much crying. I'd never been much of a crier—not until these past couple days, at least.

I was pretty sure that I'd cried more after Pitt left than I'd cried in my entire life. And there would only be more crying coming my way.

A car honked at me as I sat at a stop light, lost in thought. I pushed the gas pedal and moved ahead, trying to pay more attention to the road and the traffic surrounding me. The last thing I needed was to wreck the rental car.

At eight-thirty in the morning on a Monday, Austin traffic was a nightmare. There were cars everywhere, and the lights seemed to last forever. I hadn't even made it onto the interstate yet, not that things would move much faster there. I knew that it would be packed, too.

As I sat at another red light, my mind wandered back to one stormy night when Grampa had come to our house late. He'd banged on the door, waking us all up. It had been the one and only time I'd seen the man upset and crying.

Mom and Dad helped him sit at the dining room table, and both of them were asking him what was wrong. I had this instinct that told me what he couldn't manage to get out of his mouth. "It's Grandma," I said.

When my Grampa nodded, my parents grew even more worried. Mom asked him, "What happened, Dad?"

"I woke up," Grampa choked out. "She wasn't in bed." He buried his face in his hands. "I heard her voice coming from the living room and went to see what she was doing." He burst into uncontrollable sobs, and I found myself crying right along with him.

Reaching out, I ran my hand over the backs of his, and then he pulled his hands away from his face. "Is she hurt, Grampa?"

He shook his head. "Not anymore. She'll never feel any pain ever again."

Mom gasped, and Dad caught her as she began to fall backward. "Whoa. I've got you."

I looked at my grandfather's teary eyes and asked, "Is she dead?"

He nodded. "She got in the way of a home invasion. A man shot her. Right in the chest, he shot her."

My heart stopped beating. My mind went blank. My grandmother had been murdered. I had only been ten, and I hadn't had the mental capacity to deal with any of that.

Dad asked, "Did you call the police?"

Grampa nodded. "They'd been called by our neighbor when he saw the man breaking in our front door. Before the murderer could escape, they got him. They killed him. He wouldn't stop running away from the police. They had no choice. At least I know who did it, and that they won't ever hurt anyone ever again."

"Did they take Mom to the hospital?" my mother asked.

"They did. She was pronounced dead on arrival." He broke down again. "They took her to the morgue."

That was the only other time in my life that I had sobbed uncontrollably. Tears had streamed down my face, and I'd gone into such a state of shock and numbness that the lightning and thunder all pretty much disappeared from my notice.

Part of my mind raced to recall every memory I'd had of my grandmother, while the other part of it remained in shock. I couldn't even recall what happened after that. Bits and pieces from the funeral were all that was left of that dark time in our lives.

The light changed and I suddenly came back to myself. I looked in the rearview mirror to see that tears poured out from under my sunglasses. "More tears?" The first thing I planned to do when I got to my parents' place was guzzle as much water as I could. I needed to regain some of the water I'd lost from all the crying.

Looking at my purse, I thought about taking my cell out and turning it back on so I could call Pitt. Of course, Austin had strict laws about being on the phone while driving, and the morning traffic was awful, making it even more dangerous to make any calls—hands-free or not.

But my heart ached so badly, and I knew only one person could help me through this time.

Pitt.

I didn't know if he could even manage to come to me, since he'd been away from his ranch for so long. But I thought he might drop everything to be there for me.

The one thing I knew for sure was that I had to call him as soon as I got to my parent's home and tell him what had happened. I hoped he wouldn't be too mad at me for not being able to answer any calls he'd made to me, or answer any texts he'd sent.

Sure that he would understand once I had the time to explain things to him, I opted to leave my phone off and in my purse. The traffic was just too bad to risk it. And I was already heavily distracted as it was.

The last stoplight before the highway was just ahead. As I approached, I found I was the first in line at the light.

A sob came out of me out of nowhere, and I broke down once again. Crying and gasping, I tried my best to get myself under control. "Stop it! You've got to calm down!"

From somewhere behind me I heard the sound of a horn honking, and I thought it meant that the light had turned green. I wiped my eyes frantically as I stepped on the gas.

More horns honked—tons of them—and I had no idea what was happening. But then I heard a horn that made a deeper sound than the rest of them. In a flash of red and chrome, I finally saw why there was so much honking.

Where the hell did that truck come from?

CHAPTER 23

Pitt

"Why the long face, Pitt?" my grandfather asked me as we sat outside on his porch, watching the February snow falling in the afternoon sky.

I leaned back in the old white rocker, wishing that things hadn't turned out the way they had. "She was supposed to be here with me, Gramps. Instead, I have no idea where Kaylee Simpson is."

"You still going on about that girl, boy?" He shook his head. "You've done all you can do. You got those folks' phone number, didn't ya'?"

"I did get the Jamison's phone number." Camilla Chambers had found out who'd given Kaylee a ride to Aruba to catch a plane at the airport. "But they'd said that she didn't say much at all. So, that was a dead end."

"Well, that's a good thing they told ya' that. At least you know she wasn't kidnapped or nothing like that," Gramps offered.

"No, it doesn't look like any foul play was involved in her leaving." Tapping my fingers on the arm of the chair, I tried to think about what else I could do to try to find Kaylee. "The emergency number

Camilla gave me didn't work either. I'd called it for a solid week and never got an answer. And then one day when I called it, there was a recording telling me that the number had been disconnected."

"And didn't you tell me that emergency number was her grandfather's?" Gramps asked me as he cocked one white eyebrow.

"Yes, sir. I sure did." I looked at him to see if he had some new lead I could go with.

"Well, what if she told him he should change his number so you couldn't track her down?" His question made my heart sink.

"We were in love, Gramps." I had to keep telling everyone that, and none of them seemed to believe me.

Gramps nodded. "I'm sure you were in love. Her—I'm not so sure about. It's been six months, and the girl hasn't tried to contact you once."

But I knew she couldn't have been stringing me along. "Well, believe it or not, she did love me. She'd been waiting for the one man she would love forever. And that man was me, Gramps."

He shook his head as if he didn't believe me. "Son, let me tell you something about coming from money. Some people have a hard time with it. Some people are intimidated by wealth, and you got tons of wealth."

"I don't think she was intimidated by my money, Gramps." She'd never acted like she was, anyway.

"Maybe she wasn't happy with you being a rancher," he said as he looked at me with wise eyes.

She had expressed her opinion about that. "She asked me several times why I would still be working so hard when I had money from Dad. But I thought I'd explained my love for the work in a way that she could understand. But maybe you're right. The thing is, I want to —no, scratch that—I *need* to hear her tell me why she's done this to us."

With a huff, he said, "Doubt you'll ever get an explanation from the girl. Seems she's covered her tracks very well."

The way he phrased that gave me a new idea. "Maybe I should hire a private investigator."

"I don't think you should do that." Gramps shook his head as he frowned. "The girl doesn't want to be found. What good could come of tracking her down? Do you need her to say the words to your face? I wouldn't want to hear some woman tell me that she just didn't feel the same way I did, or that she'd run away rather than tell me that."

I couldn't believe Kaylee didn't want to be with me anymore. "She cried when I left. I saw her running and knew she was crying."

"Maybe she was running back to her place to pack up and get the hell out of there. She might've been afraid that you would change your mind and go back to the island. Maybe she wanted things to end on a note that left you happy, instead of having to see you sad that she wanted things to end."

"Maybe you're right." I couldn't deny that something had happened, even if I'd been trying my best to stay optimistic.

I got up to head back out to check on the herd. "I just have this feeling that she's not okay, and I'm afraid it won't go away until I get a chance to speak with her. What if something happened to her, Gramps?"

Turning to look back at him, I saw him shrug his shoulders. "What if something did happen to her? What could you do about that anyway?"

"Be there for her." I turned back around to head to the barn. "I think I will hire a P.I. to track her down. I can tell him not to make contact with her. I just want to know if she's okay. I have a feeling she's back in Austin, where she was working before she came to the resort."

"What if that P.I. comes back with some information that would hurt you, Pitt?" he asked me as he got up to head inside. "What if he tells you he found her, and she's with another man? I bet that would feel much worse than this does."

Nodding, I knew he was right. "I'll think about it more before I do anything. Thanks for the advice, Gramps."

Nothing made me happy anymore. I sighed, the familiar sensation of emptiness filling me. Nothing made me happy anymore, and I couldn't get over the feeling that a part of me was missing. Kaylee had become a part of me through the summer, and I didn't feel whole without her.

How could she do this to us?

There had never been a doubt in my mind that I'd gotten into Kaylee's heart, too. I could see it in her golden-brown eyes—she had truly loved me. It didn't matter that no one in my family believed me. I knew she had loved me. I didn't know if she still did or not, but she had loved me back then.

Six months had passed since I'd last seen her. Six long-as-hell months had gone by with me not knowing where she was or how she was doing. I didn't know how much more I could take of not knowing anything.

Gramps was right. If I found out that she'd moved on, it would rip my heart out. But what if I that wasn't the case? What if I found out that she'd just gotten scared and ran off?

Can I forgive her for that?

Picking up my saddle, I put it on Dusty, a new gelding we'd acquired a month ago. "Hey there, Dusty. Wanna help me check on the cattle this afternoon?"

He blew out his breath, making his lips wiggle. I took his gesture as a yes.

After tightening the cinch, I climbed into the saddle, then headed out into the snowy day. The snow-covered mountains sparkled in the sun's light. It was one of those days that I used to take pleasure in. Cold, but not bone-chilling, the air smelling fresh and soft. There wasn't any wind to speak of, making the lightly falling snow come down peacefully.

As always, my mind went to Kaylee, and I thought about how the winter in Austin was treating her. I'd taken to watching the Weather Channel to find out what she might be experiencing if she were there. I pictured her wearing something with long sleeves and a pair of jeans with boots on. Maybe a light sweater, too, as the temperature in Austin that day was supposed to be around sixty-four degrees.

As I rode out to the middle pasture, I had an idea. Kaylee was a bartender. There were lots and lots of bars in Austin. All I had to do was call each one and ask for Kaylee Simpson. If I could find where she worked, I could sneak up on her.

Well aware of how stalkerish that idea sounded, I didn't care.

Pulling my cell phone out of my pocket, I set to work. Doing a search on the internet, I was able to click on the phone numbers and make the calls.

All the rest of that afternoon, I called one bar after the other, and none of them said she worked there. Riding back up to the barn after moving the herd to the back pasture, I saw that I'd missed one on the list.

The way my stomach started to tickle had me getting excited, feeling that this would be the one. Pressing the phone number on the screen, I took a deep breath to steady my nerves. "Thanks for calling The Dogwood, Jake speaking. How can I help you?"

"Hi Jake, you can help me by letting me talk to Kaylee Simpson." I crossed my fingers for good luck. "We're old friends from high school." I figured I had a better chance of speaking to her if she didn't know it was me.

"Man, you're about a year too late for that," he told me. "She left us last May to go work on an island resort. Sorry, fella."

"So, she did work for you, but she doesn't anymore?" I asked, my shoulders slumping with disappointment.

"Yes, that's right," the guy told me. "The resort is called Paradise Resort or something like that, if you want to try to track her down there. I'm sure she would love to hear from an old friend."

So he didn't know that Kaylee had quit her job on the island. I had a hard time believing that Kaylee was back in Austin, then. "You haven't seen her around, have you?"

"No." He laughed. "Didn't you hear me? She's on an island. Paradise Resort. You find the phone number online, but that's about all I can tell you, dude. The rest is up to you."

"No, I understand. Thanks." I ended the call as worry began to seep in.

Where the hell is that woman?

If she hadn't gone back to her hometown where her family was, then where had she gone? And why hadn't I thought about getting her parents' phone number?

There were so many things I kept kicking myself about: not staying, not taking her with me, not getting phone numbers—other than her cell—that would help me get in contact with her.

Sending a private investigator to Austin to look for her sounded like a bad idea now. There was nowhere else she'd ever talked about. It felt like hell, not being able to find her.

Lucy was in the barn when I rode up. "Hey Pitt." She looked at me and must've realized I was in a bad mood. "What the hell happened to you out there today?"

She'd been big on telling me to get over Kaylee, so I wasn't sure what to say to her. "Nothing."

"Come on, Pitt," she cajoled. "You look like the wind has been taken out of your sails."

It had. But I wasn't in the mood for a lecture on how I needed to move on. "It's nothing."

"Suit yourself, stubborn." She walked out of the barn, then stopped and turned to look at me as I got off the horse. "I'm sure she's moved on, Pitt. You should, too."

Looking at her, I didn't know how to explain the way I was feeling to my family. "I'm tired, Lucy. Just leave me alone, will ya'?"

I'd never been more tired in my entire life. I'd never felt so alone, either.

Where the hell are you, Kaylee Simpson?

CHAPTER 24

Kaylee

"Kaylee...Kaylee. Kaylee, can you hear me?" a woman's soft voice called out to me.

All I could see was darkness. All I could hear were beeps and buzzing noises. And I couldn't feel much of anything.

I knew I was lying down, but that's about all I knew. When I tried to open my mouth to speak, I found that I couldn't.

Moving my arms seemed impossible, too. And then I began to panic, but only inside my head. My body wouldn't move at all.

"Wiggle your fingers, Kaylee," the woman said.

It took everything in me, but I managed to wiggle the fingers on my right hand. Then I did the same with the fingers on my left hand. Another voice—a man's voice this time—encouraged me.

"Great job, Kaylee." A hand ran over my toes. "Can you do the same thing with your toes now?"

It made no sense to me why things that had always been so easy were now suddenly so difficult. It took so much concentration to move even my smallest body parts.

Once I got my toes moving the woman praised me again. "This is going so well, Kaylee. Would you like to try to open your eyes for us?"

Oddly enough, the dark felt like home to me. Like a place I'd been for a very long time. The thought of seeing light again bothered me so much that it made it hard to do what she'd asked.

I felt myself slipping back to the deep darkness, not willing to open my eyes for anyone. Then a handsome face moved in. Blue eyes glistened, and his dark curls surrounded his adorable face. He raised one brow as his lips moved. "Do it for me, Kaylee. Open your eyes for me, baby."

He seemed so familiar, but I couldn't think of his name. I knew one thing though: I wanted to see that man.

Although my eyelids felt heavier than they'd ever felt in my life, I managed to get them to open. Everything was blurry, and it was still pretty dark. "We've kept the lights on low, Kaylee," the woman told me. "I know things are probably looking pretty blurry right now, but that will go away soon." She paused, and then added, "Hopefully."

Something ran across the bottom of my foot, and I moved my leg to avoid it. "Good," the man in the room said. "You've got feeling in your lower extremities. That's very good, Kaylee."

Little by little my vision began to clear, and I could make out the man and woman. What I saw made no sense to me. They wore blue scrubs, and it seemed like I was in a hospital bed.

How did I get here?

I wanted to ask the question, but the words wouldn't come out. My mouth wasn't working at all. I tried to move my mouth again then realized what was wrong. Something was in my mouth.

When I tried to move my arm to use my hand to remove whatever was there, I found it was strapped down. Pulling at both hands, I moaned a little, my whole body hurting with the effort.

"Easy," the man said as he came forward. "You're restrained for your own good, Kaylee."

Why?

What was going on? Why was I tied down in a hospital? Nothing made any sense.

I wanted to know where my family was. Then something in my brain told me where they were.

My grandfather is dead.

My heart pounded, and I heard the beeping noise get faster. "We're going to have to give her a sedative," the woman said.

"Hold on. Let me try to calm her down," the man told her. He came in very close to my face. "Kaylee, you have to calm down for us, okay? Let me explain what's happened to you. It's important that you stay calm, or we'll be forced to put you back under. Aren't you ready to wake up?"

I wanted to know how long I'd been asleep. I wanted to stay awake. But I wanted to be free from the restraints and have the thing in my mouth taken out so I could talk.

The woman in the room came in close, too. "Kaylee, you were in an automobile accident. You've been in a coma for twelve months now. We can't rush this. You've got to take this one day at a time."

Twelve months? A year?

I didn't understand anything. Pulling at the straps again, I moaned, trying to get them to understand that I needed them removed. The woman looked at the man who nodded back at her. "Sedate her."

I jerked my legs as hard as I could, thinking that they were free. I was wrong. They had more give than my arms did, but they were restrained as well. The more I moved, the more I realized just how restrained I was. Something ran across my stomach also, holding me down.

I needed my parents. Why weren't they there with me? And the man I'd seen in my head, where was he?

Little by little, my body stopped moving and I began to fade back into the black state. It was comfortable there in the dark. There was nothing to bother me there.

I could still hear the people in the room talking as I faded further and further back. "I think we should take the restraints off her. When she wakes again, she'll be less likely to freak out," the woman said.

"And we can take her off the respirator, too," the man added.

"That'll help. Can you call her parents and tell them they should come up here in the morning? It'll be a lot better if they're here when she comes around after this wears off."

The sound of a door opening had me listening, hanging on to consciousness, trying not to fall asleep. "And who told you that you could try to bring her around?" a man shouted.

"Doctor Wendell, sir," the woman answered him.

"He's not her doctor. I am." I heard his shoes clicking across the floor. "There's still too much swelling around her brain to try to bring her back."

"Her family has turned her over to Doctor Wendell, sir," the man told him. "They're worried about her slow progress and would like to follow his advice."

"No one has contacted me about this. She's still my patient until I hear it from her parents," he barked. "Until then, I'm her doctor, and I don't feel comfortable bringing her back just yet."

"Her family thinks it's time," she pleaded. "She is stable, the swelling has gone down, and she's missing out on a hell of a lot. I have to agree with her family on this. She needs to be brought back and start rehabilitation therapy."

Listening to these doctors discuss my condition, I wondered how I'd gotten in such a state. I remembered being on an airplane and then getting into a tiny car. Everything looked blurry for some reason. I was crying, I think. And then there were horns honking.

A red truck!

It must have hit me. I couldn't recall a thing after seeing that blur of red. And I'd been in a coma for a year.

Suddenly, I wanted to wake up. I wanted to see what I'd been missing out on.

The woman had said I was missing out on a hell of a lot of things. Could the man in my head be one of those things?

I wiggled my fingers, and then tried my best to say, "Wake up."

My eyes had closed and wouldn't open back up. But the woman had understood me. "She's trying to speak again. See, she wants to wake up, Doctor Sealy. We think it's best if we take off the restraints and the respirator. She'll be calmer without them on."

"No one does a thing until her parents contact me personally and tell me they no longer want my services." I heard the man's shoes clicking at a fast pace out of the room.

"Call her family right now," the other man left in the room was quick to say. "Tell them what they need to do."

"I'll get on that right away." I heard the woman's footsteps leaving my room.

Feeling fingers trail up my arm, I heard the man as he said, "We'll get you up and going again, Kaylee Simpson. You can count on us. You've got so much to live for. Don't worry. Sleep. Tomorrow you'll wake to a brand new day."

As he finished speaking, the medication took me under. One dream after another led to a restless sleep. The man who'd come to me in my head was there again, calling to me, telling me to come back to him.

Over and over, he kept calling to me, and I kept trying to go to him, but it was like I was stuck in thick mud that wouldn't let me go. No matter how hard I tried, I couldn't get to him, and he never moved any closer to me.

Frustration filled me. Finally, the man stopped calling out to me and turned to walk away. I tried to shout at him not to go, but nothing came out.

He walked off into the darkness, leaving me behind to stay stuck right where I was. I began to cry, feeling helpless and lost.

"Kaylee, are you okay?" a woman asked me.

My head swam as my conscious mind began to wake up. I couldn't communicate yet, but I could hear, and I could nod a little.

"Oh my gosh, she moved her head!" I heard my mother say.

My heart sped up as I thought about my parents being there, and I heard the beeping sound speed up, too.

The nurse cautioned them. "Okay, we need to keep her calm. She seems to get upset pretty easily. I don't want to have to put her back under, but if she gets overwhelmed, I'll have to. She probably won't be able to talk for a few days, maybe even longer. I don't want you to worry about that or worry her about it, either. This is going to be a slow process, to get her fully healed."

Dad chimed in, "We know that. We've educated ourselves on this kind of thing." I felt a hand on my leg, patting it gently. "We'll keep her calm. Don't you worry. We can't wait to get her home, but we know nothing can be rushed."

One voice seemed to be missing. The man's voice. The man who'd been in my dreams.

Where is he?

Slowly, I opened my eyes and saw three people standing around my bed. They were just shadows to me at first, but then very slowly they came into focus.

Tears were streaming down my mother's cheeks, and then she was leaning over me with her hands on my cheeks. "There she is. Kaylee, it's so good to see your pretty eyes open. You're going to get better. I don't want you to worry about a thing."

The only thing I was worried about was the whereabouts of the man in my head. I nodded, making Mom smile.

She moved back to let Dad lean in. He brushed my hair back as he smiled at me. "We're so happy to see you awake. We've missed you."

A tear fell from my eye as I thought about the fact that I'd missed my grandfather's funeral. Dad wiped it away then stepped back.

The nurse leaned over me next. "Kaylee, we're going to do some tests today. Nothing strenuous, so there' no reason to worry. If you feel sleepy, go to sleep. Don't fight it. This is going to take time, and you're going to have to listen to your body. We all must be patient. Your parents will be here with you every step of the way."

Good. But what about the man from my dreams? Where is he?

CHAPTER 25

Pitt

J ust as I walked outside to start my day, I saw headlights coming up our driveway. "Now who'd be up at four in the morning, besides us?"

Shielding my eyes as the car pulled to a stop in front of me, I couldn't help but smile when Galen Dunne got out of the backseat. "Mornin', stranger."

"You sure surprised me, Galen," I admitted as I shook his hand. "Morning."

"Your mother didn't tell ya' I was coming today?" he asked with a raised brow. "That's odd."

"Nope, she hasn't said a word about you coming to visit." I turned to lead him into the house, then stopped and waved at his driver. "You come on in, too. Mom'll get you boys some breakfast."

The driver waited until Galen gave him a nod, then he got out to join us. "Thanks, Mr. Zycan."

My sister Janice came out the door just as we were about to go in it. "Oops."

"Hey sis." I jerked my head toward Galen. "You remember Mr. Dunne, don't you?"

"Duh," she said then gave the man a hug. "How've you been, Mr. Dunne? We've missed seeing you around here. It's been a long time."

Galen let her go. "I've been doing well. Life treatin' you okay there, hass?"

"It sure has." She pointed at the golf cart behind us. "I've gotta get going, but I'll see you at lunch if you're still here."

"I will be here. I'm spending the day with your mother. She's gonna help me out with some things." He turned to head inside.

I decided I should stick around for a while. "Janice, tell the boys I'll be running a little late today, but not to worry."

"Sure thing, Pitt." Janice slid into the driver's seat of the golf cart, then sped away.

"What's Mom gonna help you with, Galen?" I led the men to the kitchen where I knew Mom must've been making breakfast on Cookie's day off. The smell of bacon and coffee wafted past my nostrils as we got closer to the kitchen.

"I need her advice. I think I might've met a woman who can keep me happy forever. I've been a confirmed bachelor for so long, I don't know if I can trust my own judgment. But I've never felt this way about anyone in my life." The smile he wore was priceless. "I met her this summer, at the resort." He stopped and looked at me with a stern face. "By the way, where were you this past summer? I know I invited you to come back to the island."

"Congratulations, Galen. Good for you. And I didn't go to the island this summer because I didn't feel like it." I hadn't felt like doing much of anything besides ranching.

"And why not?" Galen wasn't about to let it go.

So I told him everything. "That girl I was with, Kaylee. She left the island the same day I did, without telling me. We'd planned for her to visit me when she got her vacation, but I never heard a word from her after I left. Her cell isn't working anymore, and neither is the emergency contact number she gave Camilla. It's been a whole year—and still nothing."

We'd made it to the kitchen, and Mom was there, stirring a pan of eggs. She left the stove to give Galen a hug. "There he is."

Galen's arms spread wide. "Here I am." The two hugged, then he kissed her cheek. "Fannie, how have you been doing?"

"I've been getting by just fine." Mom went back to her cooking. "It's almost ready, boys. Pitt, you staying for breakfast too, hon?"

"Yes ma'am." I took my hat off, then went to get cups of coffee for everyone. "Coffee, guys?"

"Sure," the driver said.

"Me, too," Galen said as he took a seat at the island counter that Mom was working behind. "You're looking great, Fannie."

"Thanks. So are you." She nodded as she put the scrambled eggs in a bowl. "You do look different. Maybe it is love, Galen."

"It's hard to tell when you've told yourself all of your life that love doesn't exist." He picked up the coffee I'd placed in front of him, blowing across the top of it to cool it down.

After giving the driver his cup, I asked, "What's your name, buddy?"

"Calvin." He picked up the cup and took a sip. "Thanks."

Taking a seat, I added in my two cents. "Maybe love doesn't exist. I sure thought what Kaylee and I had was love." I took a sip of the hot coffee then put it on the bar. "But don't listen to me." I took Mom's hint by how she was glaring at me.

"Yes, don't listen to Pitt." Mom looked back at Galen. "I think he was more in love than she was."

Galen drummed his fingers on the bar. "She was an odd one, I'll give you that."

"She was fun, not odd," I defended her. "Except for the couple weeks the island doctor put her on meds for ADHD. Then she was odd—it turned her into a zombie. I made her get off them."

Mom's jaw dropped. "You did what?"

Galen shook his head. "You made her get off something the doctor had prescribed for her?"

"You didn't see her, Galen. She was a shell of her former self. And she was weak, dizzy, had no appetite at all." I knew I'd done the right thing. Kaylee had agreed with me once the fog caused by the meds had been lifted. "I won't feel bad about what I did. She needed to get off those pills. Once she did, she was back to her former self, and that's when we fell head over heels in love."

Galen pointed out, "Or so you thought, anyway."

Shrugging, I had to admit he must've been right. "Yeah. I thought we were in love. Seems only I was."

Mom served our food as she scowled at me. "You've never told me this, Pitt. This whole last year, you've never told me that you made her stop taking medication. Now I get it."

"You get what?" I asked, not having a clue where she was going with this.

"Why she ran off." She put a spoonful of eggs on my plate. "You made her do things she didn't want to. You've always been like that. Remember when you made your sister Lucy get on that bull when she was fifteen? You pushed her and pushed her until she finally got on. And what happened next, Pitt?"

"She fell off and broke her leg." I ran my hand over my face as I recalled the bloodcurdling scream she'd made that day. "But you know what else happened, Mom?"

She raised her brows, knowing exactly what else had happened. "Okay, so what? She got right back on that bull as soon as her cast came off."

"Yeah, and eventually she won seven bullriding competitions. The only girl in this whole state who's done that." I mentally patted myself on the back. "And it was all because of me."

"And her strong will," Mom added. "But that doesn't matter. We're talking about Kaylee. Maybe she couldn't figure out how to tell you that she wanted to be on those medications again, Pitt. You can be so demanding that it makes it hard to tell you things sometimes."

Sitting there, I wondered if Mom was right. Had I pushed Kaylee too hard? She'd seemed happy that I loved her just the way she was.

Galen offered his advice. "Pitt, I say move on."

"Yes, it's time to move on," Mom agreed. "It's been a year. Time to put her in the past and leave her there."

But I didn't want to do that yet. "I might hire an investigator to find her. I just want—no, I *need* to know she's okay."

"Your grandfather told me you were thinking about doing that." Mom put a couple of pieces of bacon on my plate. "I didn't bring it up, since you never talked to me about it. I figured you'd followed his good advice and put that idea out of your head."

"It's never left." I took another sip of the hot coffee. "And the more time that passes, the more it seems like the right thing to do."

"She's got your number, doesn't she?" Calvin asked me.

I nodded. "Yep."

"Well, then she doesn't want to be found," he added.

"What if she's hurt somewhere?" I asked. "I keep on thinking that she's somewhere and she's hurt, and no one can help her. Why do I keep thinking that?"

Mom huffed. "Because you can't bring yourself to imagine that she didn't love you, Pitt."

"Because she did love me." I knew Kaylee had loved me. She had to have loved me. She'd given her virginity to me. I knew how much that meant to her.

But I had made her get off those pills. There was that. I chewed my lower lip as I thought about what everyone had said. I felt terrible.

Galen picked up his fork. "This looks great, Fannie. Thanks for making us breakfast."

The three of them dug in as I kind of pushed the food around on my plate, my appetite gone. Kaylee might have loved me a year ago, but it was clear that she didn't anymore.

If she still loved me, she would've called by now. No one lets that much time pass unless they're done for good.

I knew then that I wouldn't hire anyone to go looking for her. Whatever they found would surely break my heart even more. I was already a shell of my former self. I didn't need to lose any more of what she'd left behind.

"Has anyone ever died of heart break?" I asked.

Galen quickly stated, "No, not that I've ever heard of. The best thing for you to do now is to get back on that horse."

"I suppose you mean I should get myself another girl." I didn't want another girl.

"Yes, that's what I mean." Galen put his fork down as he looked at me. "A year is far too long to be waiting around on anyone."

"Yeah, Pitt," Mom agreed. "Stop waiting around. That girl isn't coming back to you. You need to get that through your head. She has your number. If she hasn't called by now, odds are, she won't."

They were right. "Yeah, I know." Getting up, I decided to get on with my day. "See you guys at lunch."

Walking to the door, I felt the weight shift in my heart. I had to let Kaylee go. For my own good, I had to let it all go. Little by little, the love was leaving my heart, leaving deep holes behind—holes that I knew no one else could ever fill back up.

Finding someone new wasn't going to work for me. No one could ever replace Kaylee. She was one in a million. But maybe one day—in the far away future—another woman would make a place in my heart. For now, though, I wasn't going to let anyone even try.

I needed to be alone for a while. I needed time to grieve. I'd held onto the idea of finding Kaylee for so long that I hadn't grieved for the loss of her love. It was time to do that. Time to put her behind me. She had no place in my future.

Goodbye, Kaylee Simpson.

CHAPTER 26

Kaylee

A month of rehabilitation and I'd finally gained enough strength in my arms to feed myself without making a mess. "Look, Dad. I haven't spilled a bit of anything. I'm making progress."

"You are." He got up from the rocking chair he'd been sitting in. "Your mother and I have a surprise for you today. Now that you can hold things without dropping them, we think you're ready."

"Mom's coming today?" I asked with surprise. They hadn't come together to see me since that first time. "I thought you guys didn't like to leave the dog alone."

"Um, yeah." He turned away from me as he went on. "We don't really have a dog."

They lied about having a dog?

"Why would you lie about something like that?" I put the spoon down then pushed the tray away. "Why would you guys lie to me at all?"

Turning back to face me, his expression showed how distressed he was that he'd upset me. "Calm down. It's all okay. Your mother is on her way over. You'll find out about everything very soon."

"Dad, you said you have a dog." I wanted to know why they had lied about something so seemingly insignificant. "Mom said you have a dog. So if there's no dog, why is it that one of you has to stay home at all times?"

All he could do was shrug. "You'll see."

"I'll see?" With a huff, I picked up the remote to the television to turn it on, deciding to ignore him until he told me the truth.

But Dad wasn't having that, leaning over and taking it out of my hand. "I saw your mother parking the car out the window. Let's leave this off for now."

"I don't see why." Crossing my arms, I thought he was acting weird. "You're acting very weird, Dad."

"Yeah, I know I am." He walked toward the door. "I'm going to help your mom. We'll be right back."

I noticed that he'd put the remote on the table where I couldn't reach it. "Great." I was sick of being stuck in the hospital bed. I'd made lots of progress with my upper body, but my lower body would take longer to get back in working order.

And that wasn't the only area where progress was slow. The man in my head remained nameless. All I remembered was that we'd met on an island. And that we'd fallen in love. But I hadn't said a thing to my parents or anyone else about the man whose name I couldn't remember. I didn't want my parents to know I'd finally given away my virginity. There were some things parents just didn't need to know about their kids.

Though I couldn't remember his name, my memories of what happened on the island were vivid. Everything was vivid—right up until the moment the red truck came into my view.

I knew that I had been planning to visit the man I'd fallen in love with at his home. But I couldn't recall where that was either.

My parents came back in, and Dad was carrying a baby. "What's this? You guys are babysitters now?"

Mom nodded. "Yeah, you could say that."

I looked at the little girl, who had adorable dark brown curls. "She's pretty cute. Whose baby is she?"

The baby's eyes were a startling shade of blue. I couldn't pull my gaze from hers as Dad came closer to me. "We've got some great news for you, Kaylee. At least, we hope you think it's as great as we do."

Pulling my eyes off the baby's, I looked at my father. "Her eyes remind me of someone's." They were the same color as the man I thought about all the time. And her hair was the same color as his, too.

Mom took a seat on the bed then Dad handed the baby to her. "This is Karen," she said.

I reached over, running my hand through her thick curls. I couldn't help myself—it felt so natural to touch her. "That's what I called that baby doll I carried around for years."

"That's right," Mom said with a grin. "We thought you might remember that. And your father and I thought you might like us to name her that."

Now I was really confused. "Why would someone let you name their baby? You didn't adopt a baby, did you?"

Dad cleared his throat. "Okay, no more pussyfooting around. Here are the facts for you, Kaylee."

"Great. I'd like to know the facts." The baby took my finger, holding it firmly as she looked at me. "She's really cute. Like, adorable."

"I think so, too," Mom said. She looked at my father. "Let me start this out. It's a mom thing."

"I agree." He took a seat, looking relieved. "Let's get this over with."

The feeling that something was hanging heavy in the air was nearly overwhelming. "Okay, Mom. Tell me what's going on."

"This beautiful baby girl is yours, sweetie," the words came from her mouth, but my ears refused to hear them.

How in the hell can this be?

"Mom, no. There's no way this baby is mine." I looked at my father. "Dad, there's no way."

Mom put her hand on my shoulder to calm me down. "Just stay calm, sweetie. Do you remember being with someone—intimately—while you were on that island?"

I didn't want to talk to them about my new sex life. But it seemed that I had to. "Yes. But I was on the pill, Mom. This is impossible. And I was in a coma for a year, Mom. How did I give birth?"

"They performed a c-section right before she was due." She moved the baby into my arms. "You were about two months pregnant when you had the accident. They found that out right away, and it was a miracle that she survived. I don't know how you got pregnant if you were on the pill, though. Did you take any other medications while you were on the island?"

Holding the baby girl in my arms felt so right. "I took some ADHD meds for a week but they made me sick. I took a few antibiotics then, to help me get better."

Mom smiled at me. "Had you told the doctor that you were taking birth control pills?"

Shaking my head, I answered, "No, I didn't. I didn't think about it."

With a nod, she went on, "Certain medications will make others stop working if you take them at the same time. That must've been what happened. So we've got our answer to how you got pregnant, don't we?"

"I guess so." There was no way I could tear my eyes away from the baby I now knew was mine. "Oh my goodness, you're my daughter. Karen."

She smiled at me and cooed. "Aw, she loves you already." Mom put her arm around me. "She's a good baby, Kaylee—so quiet and easy to care for. You're going to love being her mother. And we'll help you. Don't worry about a thing."

My father cleared his throat, taking my attention. "So, I've gotta ask this, Kaylee. Do you know who her father is?"

"Yes, I do," I nodded. "And we were in love." Looking at the baby again, I saw him in her so much it hurt. A tear fell from my eye. "I just can't remember his name."

Dad seemed okay with my answer. "Well, that's okay. You'll remember with time, I'm sure. Then we can find him and let him know he's a father."

None of it seemed real. I'd had a baby without knowing I'd ever been pregnant. "This is incredible. You're a little miracle, aren't you?" I kissed her on the forehead, making her giggle a little. "Oh, how cute you sound." The only thing missing was the man who'd made her with me. "Mom, I've got to find him. I can see him as clear as day in my head, but I can't for the life of me think of his name."

Suddenly, my mother got this strange look in her eyes. "Was the man a guest on the island? Or maybe someone you worked with?"

"He was a guest." I couldn't say how, but I was certain I knew that much about the man who'd fathered my baby.

"Then he's rich," Mom gasped.

Nodding, I knew he had money. "He's a rancher. He didn't make his money that way, though. His father died from lung cancer, and he inherited. His dad had made a fortune from some engine thingy."

Dad stood up and began pacing. I knew he was thinking, because he paced when he wrestled with a problem. "Okay, so he was a guest of the island. He's got a ranch."

"It's not his ranch. It's his grandfather's. But he loves it. But I can't remember the name of it either or where it is. A lot of names are just kind of gone. I don't know how I can remember so much, but the names still escape me." I knew I wasn't helping at all, so I got quiet and focused my attention on my baby. "How lucky am I that I didn't have to go through any of the pain that goes along with pregnancy and childbirth?"

Mom sighed. "Very lucky. But we were nervous wrecks. Your life and the baby's hung in the balance every single minute. It was so nerve-wracking that your father and I took to drinking an entire bottle of wine at the end of every day."

Looking away from my sweet little Karen, I couldn't help but feel sympathy for my parents. "God, this must've been so hard on you two. Thank you for everything you've done." It started sinking in just how much they'd done for me. "You guys could've given my baby up for adoption." I blinked as I thought about what else could have happened. "For that matter, I'm sure you could've had them abort the baby when they found out I was pregnant."

"We'd never do any of that." Mom swatted the air as if swatting away my words. "You know us better than that."

"Yeah, you're great people." I knew then how lucky I was to have my parents. "I'll never forget what you've done for Karen and me." I laughed a little. "My baby doll has come to life, it seems." Shaking my head, I had to admit, "This is just too weird. It doesn't seem real to me."

"Oh, it's going to get real for you—and real quick, sweetie," Mom said as she patted me on the back. "You're gaining more strength every day. And you'll be caring for your baby every day, too. We're going to bring her up here to spend the day with you. You'll learn how to change her clothes, her diaper, bathe her, feed her, and love her."

I looked back at my daughter. "You look just like your daddy." Playing with her curls, I found my heart pounding in my chest. "I miss him so much."

"Well, how come you never said a word about him before?" Dad asked me.

"I didn't see the use. I can't remember his name. What good would it have done to tell you I fell in love with this guy? And where is he now?" I had no idea how to find the man who'd fathered a child he knew nothing about. "I've got to figure out how to find him. You've got to help me think. My brain is still a bit foggy."

Dad went back to pacing and running his hand over his chin. "Okay, you met him on the island. How can we get a phone number to that place so we can ask about this man? And did anyone know you two were seeing each other?"

"Everyone knew about us." I thought about how we could get in touch with the resort, and I felt like an idiot when it finally hit me. "Um, the internet. We can look up the number, and there's a manager there that should know how to contact the guy." I looked around and saw a phone sitting on a desk in the corner. "If you guys can hand me one of your phones, I can look it up. Mom, you remember the name of the place, right?"

Mom pulled out a flip-phone, and I just stared at it. "Paradise Resort. What are you looking at? It's a cell."

"Like the first one ever made." I shook my head. "Dad, please tell me that you've got a smartphone."

He only shook his head. "Mine's just like hers."

There was so much to take in that my mind was going everywhere. And then it hit me hard.

"I'm a mother." Tears began flowing like rivers down my cheeks. "I had a baby." I gasped. "I can't believe this."

"Took her a while," Dad commented.

"You hush," Mom defended me. "You know how her brain works." Patting my back, she comforted me. "There, there. You've got us. Everything is going to be okay."

But there's so much I've already missed!

CHAPTER 27

Pitt

My family always put on a haunted hayride for Halloween, and this year was no exception. But this year I just wasn't feeling it. Kaylee hung heavily on my mind still, so I headed down to Gunnison to drown my sorrows.

It had been hard living without her, but it was harder still now that I'd finally let go of the idea that we'd find each other again.

Sitting at a small table for two, I picked up one of the shots of whiskey I'd ordered and downed it. A familiar voice came from somewhere behind me, "Shots, huh?"

Tanya, my old flame, came to take a seat—though I hadn't offered —at my table. "Tanya, what are you doing here?"

"Hello to you, too, Pitt Zycan." She took a drink from the long-neck bottle she'd brought with her.

"Sorry." There wasn't any reason to be rude to her. "I'm just in a shitty mood."

"And why is that?" She brushed her blonde hair back, tucking it behind her ear.

For some reason it kind of surprised me that no one had told her about my rejected love. I felt like the whole world must've known. "So, you haven't heard about my jilted lover status?"

"Jilted?" She shook her head as she placed her beer on the table. "I wouldn't call you that. I'd call you lucky to have gotten away before you got in too deep."

"I did get in too deep." I picked up the next shot in the line of five and downed it.

"Pitt, you're not the kind of man who gets in too deep." She ran her finger over the back of my hand, which rested on the table between us.

Moving my hand to get away from her touch, I looked right into her blue eyes. "But I am the type of man to get in too deep. At least with her, I was."

I saw hurt flash in her eyes at my words. "Why not me, Pitt? Why couldn't you let *me* into your heart the way you did with this girl? This moronic girl who didn't know what she had in you?"

"Don't call her a moron." I couldn't believe I would still stick up for Kaylee after the way she'd abandoned me. Another shot went down the hatch as I mentally kicked myself for always defending the girl.

"Sorry." Tanya picked up her beer, taking a long drink as she eyed me. Putting the beer back down, she went on, "Pitt, you need to move on from this girl. She's obviously not worth your time, otherwise she'd be with you now. And I think I can help you."

One of my brows arched as I smiled at her. "You offering your companionship, Tanya?"

With a nod and a seductive grin, I had my answer. "We never did have any trouble in the bedroom. It was only outside of the bedroom that we had problems. The fact that you never took me home with you was one of those problems. You never wanted to attend any work functions with me, either. Those were the kinds of things that got in our way."

"Maybe I was wrong for treating you the way I did." That was the first time I'd heard her tell me why she found it so easy to walk away from me.

"Maybe?" She smiled. "You were definitely wrong. I'm a good woman, you know."

"You are," I agreed. "And I wasn't very good to you, was I?"

"Not really." Her blue eyes glistened, and I thought there were a few tears lurking there. "I felt more like a booty call than a girlfriend —and that just wasn't enough."

"I did have the ranch to run, Tanya." We'd had this discussion before. "Up before dawn, work until after dark. Remember that? By the time I came in, ate some dinner, then showered and changed, it was nine or ten. Drinking a few beers to wind down took another hour or so. And then I'd come see you. And I would stay the night, if you recall."

She laughed openly, dropping her head back. "Pitt, you left my house by three-thirty any time you stayed over. You never showed up until midnight. Three and a half hours once a week isn't enough to say we even had a relationship."

She was right, and I knew that. "Tanya, the fact is that we just didn't have that spark—the one it takes to make each other a priority. You can't lay all the blame on me now, girl. What about you? You could've come out to the ranch at any time. You could've come with me while I watched over the herd. You could've come over anytime you wanted to, just to hang out with me. But you didn't."

"You never asked me to." She leveled her eyes on mine.

"Should I have had to ask my girl to come over to hang out with me?" I took another shot, leaving only one more.

Shaking her head, she conceded, "We both dropped the ball. Neither one of us is any more to blame than the other. But we were good in bed. That's all I'm saying, Pitt. You need to move on. I'm not saying you should move on with me, but I can help you get out of this slump you're in. Why not come on home with me and let me show you how?"

"Because I still love her, that's why." I took the last shot and wondered why I still loved Kaylee so damn much it hurt.

"Damn, she really did a number on you, handsome." Raising her hand to signal the bartender, she called out, "Set him up, Jimmy."

"I shouldn't have anymore." I looked at the five glasses I'd turned upside down on the table in front of me.

"I'm driving you home." She pulled out a couple of twenties to pay the bartender as he placed five more shots in front of me. "I've got this."

Shaking my head, I couldn't let her pay for my drinks. "No, Tanya." I looked at Jimmy. "Put them on my tab."

Tanya wasn't giving up. She put the money into Jimmy's hand. "Take it. Don't put anything on his tab. I've got him tonight."

As Jimmy walked away, I had to ask, "Tanya, do you think you're going to get me drunk, take me home, and take advantage of me?"

With an eerie laugh, she nodded. "That's the idea."

Leaning back in my chair, I looked her over. Long legs, small waist, long blonde hair, pretty blue eyes. There was nothing not to like about Tanya. Except that we had no real chemistry, not the way Kaylee and I did.

Pulling out my cell, I did the right thing, calling my sister Lucy. "Hey, Lucy, get Janice and come get me at The Last Stand. One of you can drive my truck back home. I've had too much to drink."

"On our way, Pitt." Lucy ended the call as I looked at Tanya's disappointed face.

"Well, I can see that you don't trust me." She took a drink of her beer. "I was just kidding around with you about taking advantage of you. I hope you know that."

I didn't know that. And I didn't want to get blind drunk and do anything I would regret, either. "It's better this way."

"Sure it is." She sighed. "We can't even be friends, can we?"

"To be honest, no." I slipped my cell back into my pocket. "You weren't there for me when Dad was sick. You weren't there for me after he died. I don't see why you want to be here for me for my broken heart."

"Maybe I thought you needed me." The way her eyes narrowed told me I'd hit a sore spot. "You never needed me before, Pitt. You pushed me away once your dad got sick. You do recall that, right?"

"Yes, I do." Rubbing my temples, I thought that going out for drinks had been a bad idea. "And I shouldn't blame you for doing what I asked you to do. But I did need someone back then. And you found it so easy to walk away that I knew it wasn't you who I needed. I hadn't yet met the woman I did need."

"She sounds like a saint." She raised her brows. "Are you sure you aren't glamorizing her?"

"There's nothing glamorous about Kaylee Simpson. She's just a girl with lots of spirit." Talking about her felt good. It made my heart beat in the right way, light and free. "I'd never had so much fun in my life. She and I built a treehouse. She'd started it before I got to the island, but we finished it together. We played like kids in the water. We teased each other without anyone getting their feelings hurt. She played the best pranks, and I had to work hard to figure out how to prank her back."

"And she left you," Tanya's reminder hit me right where it counted.

"Yeah." Getting up, I headed toward the door.

"Where are you going?" she asked. "There's no way your sisters are here yet."

"I know that. I just want to be alone." I couldn't talk to her anymore. Looking at Jimmy, I let him know what I was doing, "I ain't driving nowhere. I'm just gonna sit in the passenger seat of my truck until my sisters get here to drive me home."

He nodded. "Good. It was good to see you, Pitt. Don't be a stranger."

"It was good to see you, too, Jimmy." I wasn't going to be frequenting the bar anytime soon, though. "I think it's best if I drink my sorrows away at home for now, though."

"Yep." He gave me a nod then went back to work.

Although it had been over a year—fourteen months to be exact—I still wasn't in any shape to be drinking in public. If it weren't Tanya, some other woman would find me in a weak state, and I might do something I would regret forever.

Somewhere deep inside, I had this idea that Kaylee would call me and things would get back to how they were supposed to be. I kept telling myself to let it go, but deep down, I couldn't. And I didn't want to mess things up when it happened.

As I walked out of the bar, I found snowflakes dancing in the air. The first snowfall of the year was considered the luckiest. Sticking out my tongue, I caught a few flakes on it. Maybe that would bring me the luck I needed to find my woman again.

Climbing into the passenger side of my truck, I leaned the seat back, closing my eyes and wishing like hell that my cell would ring, and Kaylee would be on the other end.

The door opening had my eyes springing open as Lucy climbed into the driver's seat. "Okay, big brother, time for you and me to have a chat."

Throwing my arm over my face, I groaned. "No."

"Yes." She put the truck in reverse and backed out of the parking lot, then put it in drive and away we went. "You see, you've gotta get over this girl. She's made you crazy. And frankly, you're a real drag to be around. You've got to get mad at her. I mean, she *left* you."

"But why did she leave me? That's what I want to know," I moaned.

"That doesn't matter. You're a great guy," she said. That made me take notice, and I found myself sitting up straight, because Lucy had never told me I was a great guy.

"Are you okay?" I had to ask.

"I'm fine." She looked at me with concern in her blue eyes. "Pitt, if that girl called you right now, you'd take her back."

"Yeah, I would," I said. There wasn't a doubt in my mind that I would take her back.

"You shouldn't." Lucy shook her head. "It's been like a year and a half."

"Fourteen months," I corrected her.

"Okay, fourteen months." She frowned at me. "Pitt, no one waits around that long for anyone. Promise me that if she does call you, that you'll tell her you've moved on. Don't give her a chance to explain a thing to you. You don't need to know why she's hurt you the way she has. I'd like to see you become the man you were before you went to that damn island. And the only way that's going to happen is if you put it into your head that you will never take her back, no matter what."

"You really think that if I set my mind on that, I'll start feeling better?" I kind of thought she might be right. Which was weird, because I hardly ever thought Lucy was right.

She nodded as she pulled into the driveway. "It's the only way, Pitt."

Well, it can't hurt to try.

CHAPTER 28

Kaylee

November twentieth was my first day home. Dad wheeled me in, as I still couldn't walk much yet. I could take ten steps, and that was something, but I still wasn't fully mobile. "It's good to have you home, sweetheart."

"Thanks, Dad. It's good to be home." It wasn't my own home, but it was better than the hospital.

Mom came to me, putting Karen on my lap. "Look who's home, Karen. It's Momma."

My baby girl put her hands on my face then I got a nice slobbery kiss from her. "Oh, I missed you, baby girl." I kissed her chubby cheek then looked for the phone. "Dad, where's your phone?"

They'd moved since I'd been back in Austin. I didn't know where anything was. Even though I was with my family, I still felt out of place.

Dad went to get the landline, handing it to me. "I suppose you're going to try to call the resort again."

"Yeah." I tapped in the number I'd memorized from having called it once a day for the last couple of months. "My guess is they closed for a little while for some reason. I've made it my mission to call every day until I get someone."

"Paradise Resort, this is Nova Christakos. How can I help you today?" a woman asked me.

My heart pounded so hard that I almost couldn't breathe. "Mom, can you take, Karen? Someone finally answered."

Mom picked up the baby as Dad went to get a pen and paper. "I'll get you something to write on, Kaylee."

"Ma'am?" the lady asked.

"Oh, sorry." I'd gotten so stirred up that it was hard to focus. "I'm looking for a man."

She laughed. "Oh yeah?"

One. Two. Three. Breathe.

"Okay, sorry, let me slow down here. I'm just a little excited. I used to work there. Not last summer, but the one before that. I know that's a long time."

"It is," she said. "So what can I help you with? And if you could give me your name, that would be great."

"I'm Kaylee Simpson. I worked at Cantina Cordova." It was funny that I could suddenly remember the name of the little bar I'd worked at. That had been lost to me all these months.

"You're the girl who up and left without telling anyone," she said. "Camilla was so worried about you."

"Yeah." I felt bad about Camilla being worried. And then I realized that I'd remembered my boss's name, too. "I'd gotten a call about my grandfather passing away. I left a note, right?" I was sure I'd left a note.

"You did, but it didn't say why you left. It was short," she told me. "So, what are you calling about?"

"I was with a man while I was there. One of the guests back then. I need to get a hold of him." I hoped there wouldn't be any rules that stopped her from giving me the information.

"I'm sorry, Kaylee, I can't do that." I heard her tapping away on what sounded like a computer keyboard. "See, we had a terrible storm that tore things up. I'm afraid we've lost all the data we had on our computers. That's why we've been closed the last three months."

I didn't know what else to do. My heart felt like it was about to burst right out of my chest. "No, Nova. I'm too close now. I need his number. Or at least his name. I was in an accident, and I've lost some of my memories. His name was one of them."

"I'm so sorry to hear that." She covered the phone up with her hand, and all I heard was muddled words as she talked to someone else. Then she came back on the line. "The owner is here with me. I told him who was calling and he knew just who you were."

"He knows him!" Excitement flooded my body. "He and the man I was seeing were friends. Does he have his phone number so I can call him?"

"He does," she said, filling me with elation. "The man you're looking for is named Pitt Zycan. Does that ring a bell?"

"Pitt!" I shouted. "Yes, Pitt Zycan! Oh Lord, thank you, thank you! You have no idea how happy you've made me!" I could feel tears of happiness spilling from my eyes.

"You certainly sound happy. Mr. Dunne said you should give Pitt a call right away. He had no idea you were in an accident. He thought you'd just run off, leaving him. Mr. Dunne's sorry to say that the last time he saw Pitt, he was telling the man that he should move on."

"No, no, I never meant to hurt him." I felt terrible and happy at the same time. "Okay, give me his number, and I'll make the call. And tell Mr. Dunne not to worry. If Pitt has moved on, I won't blame him for it. And I won't try to mess anything up for Pitt either. I love the man. I never intended to hurt him, and I won't hurt him now if he's moved on with his life. I understand. It's been a long time, after all."

"You're a better woman than I," she said.

I jotted down his number then tried to get a hold of myself before making the important call. Mom and Dad were staring at me, and it had me feeling nervous. "Um, can I take this to my bedroom, and can you guys watch Karen while I make the call?"

Mom nodded, holding her hands out for my baby. "Sure." She pointed down the hallway. "Yours is the second door on the left."

Wheeling myself to my room, I got up out of the wheelchair to sit on the bed, moving slow and steady so I wouldn't fall. I had to take a few deep breaths to relax then dialed his number, keeping my fingers crossed, hoping he'd waited for me.

Our love had been true and deep; I had faith in it. Surely, he couldn't have moved on.

"Pitt Zycan speaking," as he answered my call.

I couldn't speak. Hearing his voice shook me to my core. I tried to talk, but only my breath came out.

"Hello?" he asked. "Is anyone there?"

"Who's that?" I heard a female voice ask him.

"I don't know," he answered. "Maybe a prank call. I'm gonna hang up if you don't say something."

"Hang up, Pitt," she told him.

"Pitt," I managed to get out through a choked throat. It took everything I had not to start sobbing at the sound of his voice.

But I heard only the sound of wind blowing in the background for what seemed like the longest time. Then I heard the woman swear. "Damn! Pitt, hang up the phone."

"Kaylee?" he asked.

"Yes." My entire body trembled, and I had to wrap my arm around myself to try to stop the shaking. "Pitt, I've missed you."

"Kaylee, why?" was all he said.

"Kaylee?" I heard the woman shriek. "Hang up the phone, Pitt! Hang it up right now!"

"Pitt, who is that shouting in the background?" I had to ask. She sounded concerned about him.

"Never mind," his voice sounded shaky. "Kaylee, it's been fifteen months. You do know that, right?"

"Yes, I do know that, but—"

I had to stop talking as he interrupted me. "Kaylee, it's been too long. You didn't expect me to just wait around, did you?"

The way my heart felt—as if it was sinking inside my chest—hurt like hell. "No. I didn't expect you to wait."

"I've got so many questions," he said.

I heard the woman yelling again. "No! No, Pitt. No questions. Tell her. Tell her right now!"

"Pitt, just tell me." I closed my eyes to steady myself for what I knew he was about to say.

"Kaylee, I've moved on." Only silence followed those horrible words.

"Okay. I'm sorry. I wish you only the best, Pitt." I gulped back the knot that had formed in my throat, preparing myself to say what I thought would be the last thing I'd ever get to say to the man I loved more than life itself. "Goodbye. I won't bother you again."

"Kaylee, wait," he whispered. "Where are you? Are you safe?"

"I'm in Austin. I'm safe now." I could hardly speak as my chest filled with sobs that I couldn't hold back much longer. "If you ever want to find me, then look me up on social media. But I'll understand if you don't. I never meant to hurt you. I really do hope you have a wonderful life with her." I couldn't take anymore and had to hang up the phone then.

Breaking down, I put my face in the pillow and howled out all emotion. Anger, hostility, frustration, and fear all came out at once. It all hurt so damn bad I thought I might die.

Nothing could have prepared me for hearing Pitt say he'd moved on. Not a thing in the world would've helped me take that news any better than I had.

Mom came into my room alone. "Sweetie, did it turn out badly?"

I couldn't talk. All I could do was cry and nod my head. Her arms wrapped around me as she tried to comfort me with soft words. But nothing could console me.

Pitt has moved on.

As I lay there crying, I knew I couldn't take it. I'd thought I could, but now that it had happened, I knew I couldn't. "I should've died in that accident."

Mom jerked me up by my shoulders, making me look at her. "I never want to hear you say those words again, Kaylee Simpson! I know this hurts, but you lived, and you have a beautiful little girl that you have to live for. Both of you are gifts from God. Never think that any man is worth dying over. There are other fish in the sea, you know."

"Not for me, there aren't." I fell back to the pillow.

She only pulled me back up, and I saw through blurry eyes that Dad had come in with Karen. "Sweetie, you've got her to live for now," he echoed Mom's words. "Don't give up just because you've lost her father."

"Did you tell him about her?" Mom asked.

I shook my head. "No. He was with another woman. I didn't want to ruin things for him. We'll be okay without him, I guess."

As I wiped my eyes, I caught my parents looking at each other. "Sweetie, he needs to be told about his daughter," Dad ventured. "Whether you two are together or not, he needs to know he has a child."

"I can't tell him right now." I sniffled and looked for some tissue.

Mom grabbed a box off the dresser then handed them to me. "Thanksgiving is right around the corner, and then there's Christmas after that. How about we give you until the start of the new year to tell him about her? But if you haven't told him anything by January, then your father and I will. He deserves to know, Kaylee."

"And once he does know, then what?" I looked back and forth at them. "He's rich, remember? He can take her away from her cripple of a mother and raise her with that other woman. No. Thank. You."

Had they thought anything through before coming to me with this threat?

CHAPTER 29

Pitt

Thanksgiving had always been a big deal at our house. Since Dad had had the mansion built, the entire family would come from all over the United States to stay for the four-day holiday weekend. The morning before Thanksgiving, I got up at four—as usual—and headed out to start my workday. Ranching never stopped for any holiday.

Since Kaylee's phone call, I hadn't been able to get much sleep at night. All I could manage was an hour or two at the most. Lying to the girl just didn't sit well with me.

And telling her that I'd moved on—that was a lie. I knew what she would think, hearing another woman's voice. And I'd let her believe it.

Lucy came up behind me, putting her hands on my back and pushing me along. "Come on, cowboy. Let's get a move on. We've gotta get those cattle taken care of so we can visit with the family. We only get to see them once a year, so no dilly-dallying."

I stopped and turned to look at my sister—the person who'd been there with me when Kaylee had called. "Something about what I did feels wrong."

"You mean about what you told that girl who dumped you?" She put her hands on her hips. "Pitt, you did the right thing. Think about it. She called you right before the holidays. She wants to get back together so she can get gifts. She's a moneygrubber is all she is."

Fire shot through me. "She is not! Take that back, Lucy."

"No." She turned and walked away from me.

"She never wanted my money. She's not after money," I shouted out to her.

Stopping, she turned to look at me. "Then why's she calling you all of a sudden, out of the blue?"

"I don't know." The call had only been a couple of days ago. I hadn't really had the time to analyze anything. "I need to talk to her again." It was the right thing to do. "I need to tell her that I lied."

Lucy looked shocked. "And let her walk all over you? You're crazy. You really are."

"Maybe I am." I turned to go back to my bedroom. "I'm not just going to call her though. I'm going to do more than that."

"Where're you going, Pitt Zycan?" Lucy shouted out after me.

"Don't worry about it." I could've kicked myself for listening to Lucy. Why had I let her convince me that this was the best thing to do for myself? If it had been the right thing to do, then why couldn't I eat, sleep, or think about anything other than Kaylee?

Throwing my suitcase on the bed, I packed enough clothes to last me a week. I wasn't sure why, but I wanted to give us enough time to really talk things out. I didn't know how I would take it if she'd been with another man, but I knew I had to see her. I had to touch her, smell her sweet scent, if only for one more time.

Calling the pilot for our private jet, I got him on his way to the airport to get it ready for the trip. I walked through the kitchen where Mom was already up, making breakfast for the whole family with a few of her sisters.

"Morning, Mom." I kissed her cheek. "Morning, ladies."

She looked at the suitcase in my head. "Going somewhere?"

"I'm going to Austin. My girl called me a couple of days ago. Only Lucy knows about that." The shocked look on Mom's face was priceless. "Yeah, I know. Me, confiding in Lucy, right? What a mistake. Or at least I hope it was. I told Kaylee that I'd moved on. But I'm going to see her to tell her that I lied about that. And I'm gonna tell her that I still love her, too, and see what she wants to do about that."

Aunt Linda smiled at me as she patted me on the back. "How exciting. Go get her, cowboy."

Mom looked at her sister with narrowed eyes. "This girl left my boy without a word, Linda. I'm not so sure he should go get her."

"Let him do what he feels he has to, Fannie," Aunt Linda chided her younger sister. "And give him your blessing, too."

Mom sighed. "Okay, you've got my blessing, Pitt. You taking the jet?"

"Yeah, I've got Pete getting her ready now." I started to leave then felt a hand on my shoulder.

"Where do you think you're going without giving your momma a hug, boy?" Mom turned me around and wrapped me in her arms. "I love you, Pitt. And I wish you the best of luck. You call me as soon as you hit the ground safely. And if it turns out this girl has a good reason for what she's done, I'd love to meet her."

"Great." I left feeling hopeful that everything would turn out better than it had when I'd left the island.

As I sat in the hangar, waiting for the jet to get fueled up, I searched for Kaylee on social media, finding her easily. I was surprised to find her address on her profile, but was too excited to question why she'd put it there. I didn't try to friend her. I wanted to surprise her. Plus, I didn't want to give her time to hide anyone she might have been with.

Browsing through her Facebook page, one thing stuck out. She'd only opened the account a month earlier, and she only had her mother and father as friends.

Still a loner.

There was nothing on her relationship status, and that had me feeling optimistic. And with no guy on her friend list, I felt even better.

Pete waved at me, and I went to get on the jet. Although my heart was filled with hope, there was a part of it that stayed cold, trying to protect it. I tried to remind myself that Kaylee had stayed out of my life on purpose for fifteen long, hellish months. There had to be a reason for that—and I might not like the reason.

Snow began falling not long after we started our flight. Pete got on the speaker, "Pitt, we're going to have to stop at the Denver airport and wait this out. The radar shows that it shouldn't be more than a few hours."

"A few hours?" *Shit.*

There wasn't anything anyone could do about the weather, so I tried not to let it bother me. Once we'd stopped in Denver, I went inside the airport to get something to eat. It had been two days since I'd put anything real into my stomach. I didn't want to get to Kaylee just to pass out from hunger.

The hamburger I ordered at a small café hit the spot. I dipped a fry in some ketchup and looked up just in time to see Tanya smiling at me as she walked my way. "Hey, handsome. Where you headed to?"

The way my heart stopped bothered me. I didn't want to tell her where I was going at all. I feared she would tell me the same thing my sister had. "Just going on a little trip is all. Business."

"The day before Thanksgiving?" She took a fry from the plate, dipped it in my ketchup, and then ate it.

"Yeah, it's a spur of the moment thing. Just came up." I pushed the plate away, not feeling hungry anymore. "You can have the rest. I'm done."

She looked at the half-eaten burger with one raised brow. "You're through?"

"Yep." Looking over her shoulder, I saw my pilot waving at me. "Looks like the snow has lifted. I've gotta get going." I got up and started walking away.

"Where are you going, Pitt?" Tanya asked.

"Texas," that's all I said.

"Wanna know where I'm going?" she asked.

"Nope." I kept on walking, not wanting to talk to her anymore. If she knew what I was doing, she'd give me a lecture that would only serve to piss me off.

"I'm going to Dallas," she called out. "Might've been nice to know you were heading that way. I could've hitched a ride with you on your jet, instead of paying an arm and a leg to get a seat in coach."

Not wanting to delay any longer, I waved goodbye and kept on going. "See ya', Tanya."

Once we got going again, the flight was stopped three more times due to snow, then ice, then sleet. I could've seen it as fate stepping in my way, but I chose not to.

We got to Austin around three in the morning—not a time one goes to see an old flame. I rented a hotel room and tried to get some sleep before heading to see her the next day.

Maybe it was being in the same city as Kaylee, I didn't know, but I managed to sleep until the sun woke me up. Getting up, I started the coffee maker before getting into the shower. All shaved and dressed, I gulped down the coffee, then headed out to the rental car I'd picked up at the airport.

I had the address pulled up on the GPS and was on my way to see Kaylee. My heart wouldn't slow down. I knew I was gonna pick that girl up in my arms the moment I saw her again and swing her around until she squealed with laughter.

Whatever had happened to tear her away from me would fade away for us both. Or so I prayed. Once we were together again, I was certain she would love me like she had back then.

She has to.

Stopping at a small store, I picked up bottles of red and white wine. It was Thanksgiving, and I couldn't very well show up empty handed. I had no idea what I would be heading into. Maybe she wouldn't even be home.

Stop that!

I had to think positive. If she weren't home, I'd adjust my plans. That was all it would take, some minor adjustments.

The GPS told me I was three minutes away from my destination. Only then did I think about how dumb it was for her to have put her address on her profile.

That's just asking for trouble.

Then I thought she might've done that just for me. She hadn't added any other friends, other than her parents. It was a thought that gave me comfort.

I took the last turn onto the street she lived on. Looking out the window, I stopped breathing as I looked from one house to the next, searching for the numbers on the houses.

Six more.

Only six more houses, then I would be at hers. It was a busy neighborhood, the houses squeezed right up against each other. Tons of cars were parked in driveways and along the curbs on both sides.

I had no idea what kind of car Kaylee drove. I had no idea what Kaylee had been doing in Austin. I knew she hadn't been tending bar anywhere, at least. I'd called every bar listed in the city.

Parking across the street behind a Ford Bronco, I could see the house with the address Kaylee had listed on her profile. I turned to get the bottles of wine off the passenger seat. When I turned back, I saw someone coming out the front door.

Kaylee in a wheelchair with a baby on her lap. "I need some fresh air, Mom."

I couldn't look away from her. She ran her hand over the baby's head then kissed her cheek.

It seemed she'd had an accident—and a baby, too. I had no idea why she'd called me then. She'd clearly met someone else.

She really had moved on.

CHAPTER 30

Pitt

The heat from the kitchen along with the fire in the fireplace had gotten to me, and I needed to cool off. Putting a sweater on Karen, I took her out on the front porch with me to get some fresh air. The temperature was in the mid-sixties—too warm for the fireplace to be going—but Mom had insisted Dad build a fire for the holiday.

Sometime later that afternoon, some of our family would be arriving to spend Thanksgiving with us, and Mom was cooking her heart out in the kitchen.

I'd offered my help, but I still couldn't stand for long periods of time, and the wheelchair got in her way. So, I helped by taking care of the baby and staying out of her way.

The sound of the screen squeaking open alerted my mother to the fact that someone was leaving the house. "Who's going where?"

"I need some fresh air, Mom," I called out as I wheeled my baby and me out the front door.

"You'll need a blanket if you're taking Karen out there," she called out. "Let me bring you one."

I didn't think it was cold enough for a sweater and a blanket, but Mom did, so I knew Karen would get both. I ran my hand over my baby girl's head, then kissed her cheek. "Your Grammy is so overprotective, isn't she?"

The sound of a car gunning its engine had me looking up, and I saw a black sedan pulling out from behind the old Ford Bronco that never left the parking spot on the other side of the street.

Blinking, I couldn't believe what I saw. "Pitt!" I waved my hands, but he kept going.

Mom came out with the blanket. "What did you say?"

"Mom, it's Pitt. I saw him." I watched as he sped away as fast as he could down the street. It wasn't too fast as there were lots of cars parked everywhere. And then there was a stop sign ahead. "Mom, can you catch him?"

She flew off the porch, running full speed, which was so much faster than I ever thought she could manage. "I'll catch him."

I couldn't breathe until she caught up with him at the stop sign. He rolled his window down, and I saw they were talking. Then Mom turned and waved at me as his backup lights came on, and he backed down the street, parking right in front of our house.

Dad came out the front door. "What's all the ruckus out here?"

"Dad, it's Pitt!" I handed him the baby, then pushed myself to stand up and took slow steps toward the car.

Pitt got out and came running to me, his arms spread open. "Baby! Oh, God, I'm so sorry." His arms closed around me as he lifted me off the ground, and I felt his chest shaking as he cried. "Kaylee, I had no idea. I never would've told you that lie if I'd known. Please forgive me, baby. Please."

"I forgive you." I cried as I held on to him as tightly as I could. "I love you."

"Baby, I love you, too." He kissed the side of my head. "You have no idea the hell I've lived through since that day I left you on the island. And I had no idea the hell you'd gone through. I never want to be apart from you again."

I thought my heart might pound right out of my chest. "I never want to be apart from you, either."

He carried me up the stairs to the porch then placed me back in my wheelchair. We wiped our eyes and sniffled, and then my mother introduced herself. "Sorry for how I came up on you, Pitt. My name is Phyliss Simpson, and this is my husband, Jack. And this little thing here is your daughter. We named her Karen."

Pitt's hands shook as he reached out to take his daughter for the first time. "Hey, Karen. It seems that I'm your daddy." Tears flowed down his cheeks, making mine come right back as I watched him take his daughter in his strong arms.

Our baby touched her daddy's face for the first time, and then she leaned in and gave him a slobbery kiss right on his cheek.

"She loves you already," I said as I cried. "We've missed you so much, Pitt. I talk to her about you all the time. I tell her how much I love her daddy."

"And your daddy loves your momma, sweetheart. Daddy loves you, too, pretty girl." Pitt looked at my father. "I aim to marry your daughter, Mr. Simpson. It would make me feel better if I got your permission first."

Dad laughed. "First thing. You call me Jack. No mister and missus around here, son. And it would do me a great honor to become your father-in-law." Dad shook Pitt's hand, and Mom started to cry then, too.

"Maybe we should all go inside, so the neighbors don't have to witness all this," she coaxed us.

After the Thanksgiving meal and telling my family about everything that had happened, Pitt took our daughter and me to his hotel room to spend the night. After rocking our daughter to sleep, he put her in the crib they'd brought before climbing into bed with me. "I've got a call to make. I promised my mother that I would let her know how things went."

After calling her number, he handed the phone to me. "Tell her who you are and what happened."

"Pitt, no." I felt weird doing that. He only nodded, then put the phone in my hand.

"Hello?" his mother said.

"Um, Mrs. Zycan, this is Kaylee Simpson." I looked at Pitt for a little help.

He only shook his head as his mother asked, "So, what happened, Kaylee?"

After telling her my story, she started crying and told me how happy she was that Pitt had found our baby and me. She looked forward to meeting us and told me to call her Mom.

Handing him the phone back, I wiped the tears out of my eyes. "She's happy."

"I bet she is." He put the phone down then moved his hand up and down my arm. "Care to get back to where we were before we left the island, baby?"

It was as if he'd read my mind—my body was on fire for the man. I didn't know how much longer I could wait. "First thing you need to know is that I am on birth control pills. And I haven't taken anything else to get in the way of them. So, we shouldn't make a baby, but if we do, then we do."

"Okay." He laughed a little. "It's good to have you back where you belong, Kaylee. Back in my arms, in my bed, and in my life. And thanks for adding that little cutie in the crib, too. She's a Godsend, isn't she?"

"I like to think so." I moved my hands up his muscular arms. "I've missed these guns, baby."

"I bet you have." He stared at me for a while, our eyes telling each other that everything would be alright now that we'd found each other again. Then he moved slowly until our lips met.

My body melted into his and I felt that connection again—like he and I were one. He was my home. I finally realized why I hadn't felt comfortable in my parents' home. Pitt was my home. Wherever he was, that was where I was meant to be.

Although my body was still mending, every nerve had come to life as our skin touched. Every move he made fueled the fire that burned inside of me. He rolled over, putting his body over mine then pushing my legs apart. Sinking into me, we both groaned with relief.

"Damn, I missed this," he whispered. "Being inside of you, feeling you underneath me, kissing your sweet lips. I've missed it all. That's never going to happen again."

Holding his handsome face between my hands, I just looked at him as we lay there, connected. "I have dreamt of you for so long. And to have you here with me feels surreal. To have our baby lying in a crib at the foot of our bed feels like something out of a fairytale. You really are my sweet prince, do you know that?"

His smile took my breath away. "I know that I love you and I always will. I know that I am changing your last name and our daughter's as soon as possible. And I know that we will be the happiest family in the history of families. Do you believe me?"

He moved a bit, slipping deeper into me. I ran my foot up the back of his leg. "I do believe you."

His mouth came back to mine, and our kiss took on a life of its own.

We'd known passion. We'd known desire. But we'd never experienced this much.

Both of us knew what we'd almost lost. It was evident that neither of us would ever take the other for granted. Nor would we risk the happiness of the family we'd created by doing anything to jeopardize it.

His mouth moved off mine, trailing up my neck before biting me playfully. "You're going to be a great rancher, Kaylee. So is our daughter. And one day our son will be, too."

I laughed. "How many kids are we having, Bid Daddy?"

He thrust hard as he pulled his head up to look at me. "I don't know yet. My plan is to keep you barefoot and pregnant most of the time."

I knew he was joking. "Oh, yeah?" I bucked a little. "Not if I don't let you ride me, cowboy."

"Go on and buck, girl." He pecked my lips. "I like it."

Laughing, I tried not to think about the past. But it came to my mind anyway. "Can you believe we were pregnant, Pitt? We didn't even know it, but we had a baby coming."

"And then you nearly got killed, but somehow our baby survived." He looked up at the ceiling. "God, I think I've forgotten to tell you, thank you for all you've done. You kept my family safe for me. I'll take it from here."

"I do feel safe with you." I pulled him back to kiss me. There was no place I would've rather been, than with him.

Our bodies moved together, reclaiming ownership of each other. The fact that he'd waited for me—even when he'd thought I'd run off on him—made me love him that much more.

Our love was real. Our love was true. Our love was unbreakable.

My cowboy had saved me once more. And this time, he would keep our daughter and me safe for the rest of our lives. Of that, I had no doubt.

The next day we would go to meet his family and make his home ours, too. It seemed almost too good to be true that everything had finally come together for us.

So much time had passed. So many wrong ideas had come into both our heads. But now it was clear as a Colorado sky—we'd found our happily ever after.

The End